BLOOD
SECRETS

SHAY LACY

author of *Secrets and Lies* and *Hero Needed*

CRIMSON ROMANCE

F+W Media, Inc.

Published by
Crimson Romance
an imprint of F+W Media, Inc.
10151 Carver Road, Suite 200
Blue Ash, OH 45242. U.S.A.
www.crimsonromance.com

ISBN 10: 1-4405-6713-1
ISBN 13: 978-1-4405-6713-1
eISBN 10: 1-4405-6714-X
eISBN 13: 978-1-4405-6714-8

This is a work of fiction. Names, characters, corporations, institutions, organizations, events, or locales in this novel are either the product of the author's imagination or, if real, used fictitiously. The resemblance of any character to actual persons (living or dead) is entirely coincidental.

Cover art © istock.com/MaxFX; 123rf.com/Yuriy Kirsasnov; 123rf.com/subbotina

This book is dedicated to the man who has stood by my side for more than thirty years, the original Michael. I base most of my heroes on him because I want them to embody the traits I love in him. It makes it easier to fall in love with them. Honey, I can't thank you enough for the best summer and fall ever as we walked for health while plotting my next novel together.

To the other people who stand by me: my ACC friends, the members of Maumee Valley RWA, my fellow Panera Prison inmates, my critique partner Ray Wenck, and to my squeezable friends Constance Phillips and Jenna Rutland.

Life isn't just about taking delight in the journey, but in the people who share the journey with you.

CHAPTER 1

Miami 2006

Ileana Alvarez Calderon came face to face with the man fated to be her lover, a man she'd seen only in a dream.

As she stepped out of the tropical Miami heat and into the dim warehouse, her body came alive and achingly aware of him. He stood talking to a young African American woman, turned slightly away from her. Ileana used the opportunity to catch her breath and study him, this familiar stranger. His navy slacks and light blue dress shirt showed off a long, lithe runner's body. There was an aura about him of ruthless control, from his cropped sable hair to the suit and tie he wore during Miami's sweltering summer. Whatever the woman was saying displeased him because his lips were pressed together, his jaw muscles bunched, and his posture rigid.

Protestations of denial surged inside her. This uptight man was not who she'd seen in her dream bed last night. That man's fierce passion had driven them both to a shattering climax. Of course, that had only happened in her vision. But she had the *Sight*. All her dreams came true.

Even if they defied logic and reason.

In the darkened bedroom of the dream, she'd assumed her lover was Cuban like her, but this man was white, a man her immigrant Cuban parents would not tolerate touching her. Why had the Sight selected someone so unsuitable? Who was he?

She'd come to Citadel Import-Export to procure merchandise for her family's chain of souvenir shops, not to ogle the man of her dream. If she could slip by him, maybe she could delay their meeting.

But that chance evaporated as someone entered the building behind her and she was forced to step away from the doorway.

"Excuse me." A man squeezed past her and disappeared into the cavernous building.

Her dream man's face swung her way and his dark eyes assessed her in a glance. She felt it as a physical touch. "Can I help you?" Her would-be-lover had a smooth baritone that played up her spine like an instrument.

Ileana swallowed, her throat suddenly dry. "I'm from the Calderon Consortium. I'm here to look over the newest tourist merchandise for our retail stores."

One dark eyebrow lifted. "I usually deal with Esteban Calderon." He moved towards her, his stride easy and assured.

"My father is retiring. I'm in line for succession."

He held out his hand to her. "I'm Michael Ziffkin. I own Citadel Import-Export." He was the top man himself.

"Ileana Alvarez Calderon."

She took his hand and anything else she might have said was lost as an electric thrill ran through her. The warmth of his body traveled through his hand to hers. She inhaled his clean male scent. Her head buzzed with white noise. Michael's hand tightened on hers, his chocolate brown eyes widened fractionally and his nostrils flared.

She knew she would make love with him. And she wouldn't lie docilely beneath him because the Sight decreed this was meant to be. Instead, she'd revel in his passionate loving, *yin* to his *yang*.

"Welcome to the Citadel. I look forward to working with you." His eyes warmed with appreciation as he looked her over once more. His lips kicked up at the corners, not quite a full-fledged smile.

Ileana's stomach gave a funny flip. "My succession isn't assured yet. My distant cousin, Juan Carlos Herrera, is also in line for my father's job." Why had she told him that? He didn't need to know personal matters.

A slight frown marred Michael's brow. "But he's not a Calderon and you are."

"He's blood."

"Ah, family." His tone went flat and his face smoothed into an unreadable mask. Before she could speculate any further, he offered, "I'll show you the new merchandise."

Michael turned and led the way down an aisle lined with metal shelves reaching nearly to the ceiling, filled with wooden shipping crates. She caught herself admiring the way his trousers shaped his tight rear and flushed. She moved to his side where his other temptations taunted her.

He flicked her another warm glance. "Your father is a young man. Business must be good if he's retiring early."

Michael was fishing for information. Ileana debated the wisdom of telling him the truth, but her father was stepping down so what could it hurt?

"My father has uncontrolled high blood pressure. His doctor advised him to take it easy. My mother insisted he step down."

"I'm sorry to hear that." The words rang with sincerity and something darker.

"My father's a smart man. He's taken the first steps to ensure we'll have him in our lives for a long time."

"This way." Michael stepped in front of her.

His curt reply and sudden movement brought her up short in the aisle. What had she said? She stared after him and saw how rigid his spine was, how his stride had become nearly a stalk. Had he lost his own father to a health problem?

Ileana caught up to him when the aisle widened into an area full of opened crates.

"Here," he said.

She laid her hand on his forearm. When he looked into her eyes it was nearly a physical connection. His brown eyes had darkened with what she thought was pain. Was that the reason the Sight had chosen him?

"I'm sorry if I said something wrong."

Michael gently removed her hand. "No need to apologize. I have to get back to my office soon. Please look at our most recent arrivals. I'm sure you'll find something the Calderon Consortium wants."

She'd found something she wanted all right. Her body thrummed with the need to press against Michael Ziffkin until he eased his pain inside her. She'd thought their affair would be a one-night stand, an anomaly in her life the same as her letting a white man touch her. Perhaps she'd misread the dream and they'd be together longer. So she let his curtness roll off her.

They inspected the contents of crates from Indonesia, Burma, Malaysia, Turkey, and Korea. Some of the goods would sell well in her family's tourist shops. Other items looked cheap or were too strange for their stores.

Choosing was simple—she'd worked in the family business since she was a child and knew what the stores carried. She also knew what sold well. The hard part was deciding how much product to buy and choosing items to help Calderon modernize; items she wasn't sure her father would like.

Ileana stood beside Michael, feeling the warmth of his body. He was only four inches taller than her five foot eight. She liked being nearly eye to eye with him and being close to him. His hands riveted her gaze as they touched the merchandise and then wrote firmly on the order form.

He spoke smoothly with confidence that demonstrated a firm grasp of his business and an intelligent mind.

Sight or no Sight, she found herself falling under his spell, tingling as his gaze slid up and down her body. His eyes smoldered with his bold appraisal, telling her he wasn't unmoved by her close proximity.

When their business was concluded, Ileana held out her hand. Michael grasped it and she felt that electric thrill once more.

"We'll deliver the goods this week," Michael promised. "I hope you succeed your father so we can work together more."

"Thank you. I hope so too."

Still he held onto her hand. His dark gaze pierced hers. "Would you have dinner with me?"

Ileana's breath clogged in her throat. Dinner. With a strange man, not one of her many relatives. She opened her mouth to politely refuse, but no words came out. How could she explain? Could she explain? She found she didn't want to refuse.

Unfortunately, she took too long to reply. Michael's face wiped clean of all expression. He released her hand. "I've put you in an awkward position where you don't know how you can refuse without hurting our business relationship. I'm sorry. I don't make a habit of asking customers out."

She rushed to allay his fears. "I'd like to have dinner with you. We can get to know one another as business associates."

Michael blinked. He looked like he swallowed any questions he had. "Is seven o'clock all right? Would you like to bring your boyfriend?"

"I'm not dating anyone. Where would you like to meet? I'd prefer it to be away from Little Havana." And her many prying relatives.

"The Wharf Restaurant on Market Street has great seafood."

"That sounds wonderful. I'll see you at seven."

Michael still stared at her with his serious, intent gaze. She found herself wondering what his lips would taste like. She wet her own. He tracked the movement like a predator studied prey. The compulsion to kiss him was nearly overwhelming. She felt flushed.

When he moved a little closer to her, she had difficulty breathing.

"Is there something else you want?" he murmured.

Mother of God, yes! It had been a lifetime since she'd wanted a man's hands on her, or his lips touching her in ways that wrung gasps of pleasure from her. It had been equally as long since she'd touched a man where only a lover could and heard him groan his need.

Yet Michael wasn't her *novio*, her future intended husband, to whom she could give herself. He wasn't anything to her except fate's promise. She couldn't tumble into his bed after no more than a handshake.

Ileana backed away. It was extremely hard to move. When she was a few feet from him, she whirled and walked towards the door. But she couldn't resist one last look at him over her shoulder. He wasn't a beautiful man, and yet he made her heart race, her stomach quiver, her breasts ache, and her hands itch. She'd hold off fate for as long as she could until she could get to know this quiet, almost stern man. As the door closed, she found she could breathe once more.

• • •

Michael took a deep breath and tried to calm his pounding pulse. He had no hope of taming his stiff hard-on for the next few minutes. He throbbed with need as he watched Ileana's tight ass turn the corner and glimpsed one last view of her shapely breasts.

Ileana was a siren and no matter how hard he shook his head he couldn't dispel her effect on him. She was hot. She'd made him hot. That thin crocheted top had clung to her slender body. Her full breasts had strained against the delicate material. He broke into a cold sweat imagining them unbound against his bare chest.

She was a Latin beauty with dark brown hair, a triangular face, and lips made for kissing. She spoke with the slightest Hispanic accent, her words liquid and sultry. He wanted to know what else she could do with that mouth.

Michael felt as horny as some fifteen-year-old boy. As randy as his brother Charlie used to get when their next-door neighbor walked by in her Catholic school uniform. Michael wondered if Ileana had gone to Catholic school, since most Cubans were Catholic. And had she kept her uniform for sentimental reasons? He had to squash that thought before he embarrassed himself.

He wasn't even supposed to be at this warehouse. His assistant had called to say merchandise was missing. If he hadn't taken a personal interest, he wouldn't have met Ileana. He didn't believe in fate. Not anymore.

But Ileana was a contradiction with her bold, cat-slanted brown eyes and refusal to make dinner a date. How would she have responded if he'd told her he wanted to take her home to bed? Right now. Her eyes signaled yes, but her mouth said no. He didn't understand it.

Michael shook himself like a Labrador after a swim. He'd never felt this hot for a woman. She was a customer, for God's sake. What kind of an impression had he made on her? He made a mental note to research her family's business. He was going to need all his wits about him—and all his facts—if he was going to have a business meeting with Ileana.

Thoughts of the fiery Latina dissolved when he met with his assistant once more. Desiree Carver had worked for him for four years and had made herself indispensable. He trusted her to find out what had happened to the merchandise.

He'd hired the young African American woman with the perfect skin as a favor to his best friend from college, Jamal Blake. Jamal and Desiree lived together with their young son. She'd taken to the job like a natural and now she loved Citadel almost as much as he did.

"I'll keep looking here if you want to go back to the office," Desiree told him. She had beautifully expressive liquid brown eyes.

"If it's theft, we have to get the police involved," Michael reminded her.

"I know, Michael." Her bright eyes searched his. "That woman was from Calderon?"

"One of the heirs apparent. Esteban is stepping down."

"Do we risk losing a client when that happens? She's a lot younger than him."

"She seemed pleased with our selection. She even bought some of the less traditional tourist items we just received."

Desiree smiled and nodded her satisfaction. "We'd better hope she inherits Esteban's job, then."

Michael silently agreed. He was eager for seven o'clock to arrive.

He drove through the congested streets of Miami to his office in the business district. It was centrally located to all four of his warehouses and he'd moved into the space when he'd opened his latest warehouse. He drove into the underground parking garage, relieved to be out of the scorching July sun.

Home again.

He'd spent more time at Citadel the past few years than he had in his condo. He wasn't a workaholic, but with the exception of his parents and Jamal, he had no other intimates. His brothers Rick and Charlie had lost touch with him after their brother Billy was murdered two-and-a-half years ago. They'd both returned to Miami this past winter, but he hadn't seen either of them for any length of time. That would change at Charlie's wedding in a few weeks.

Michael rode the elevator up to the eighteenth floor. Citadel's secretary/receptionist, Nadine Hutton, handed him his phone messages. From her personnel forms, he knew she was twenty-four and unmarried, but he hadn't tried to learn more about the petite brunette in the year she'd been with Citadel. He knew she was good at her job, and he paid her enough to keep her from leaving.

"If Desiree calls, please put her through no matter what."

"Sure, Michael."

Citadel's headquarters consisted of the reception area and two offices. Imported items from their warehouses made the space inviting and achieved a mix of comfortable elegance and exotic mystique. He didn't like wasting overhead, but Desiree had convinced him of the necessity once they reached their current size.

Michael entered his office and stood for a moment staring out the floor-to-ceiling window at the small patch of blue that was the Atlantic Ocean. The view was truncated by another skyscraper, but he didn't mind. His goods traveled over that blue to his warehouses and moved via truck and plane to his clients. Business was good this year. He was getting steadily wealthier, investing enough in the business to continue its growth, but diverting enough into secure funds.

He perused his messages. Security salesman, office supply salesman, a janitorial service. The fourth message was from his mother. He phoned her back first. "Hi, Mom. How are you feeling?"

"The same as yesterday. I love your concern, but can't you ask me what I'm doing instead of how?"

He hadn't been able to focus on other facets of her life since she'd been diagnosed with breast cancer a year ago. Even after six months in remission, her doctor still considered her recovering. And so did Michael.

"I'm more than my cancer, Michael," she reminded him.

"I know, Mom." He forced a smile and lightened his tone. "What are you doing?"

"I'm planning a dinner for Charlie and Juliana. I wanted to know if you could come. You've barely met Juliana."

"Mom, I grew up next door to her. I don't have to get to know her."

"You only knew her until she was sixteen. She's grown since then."

His gut tightened. "Okay, I'll get to know her. When?"

"Tonight."

"Tonight? Mom, I can't. I'm having dinner with a client."

"Can't you reschedule?"

He'd do nearly anything to make her happy, but he wanted to see Ileana again. He wouldn't give that up. "Can't Charlie and Juliana come tomorrow night?"

"They're booked until the wedding. I'm lucky I got this slot."

Anger erupted in him. His mother hadn't told her youngest son about her cancer because of his upcoming nuptials. She wanted his big day with his childhood sweetheart untroubled. Michael disagreed. Why should his mother have to pretend she felt well if she didn't?

"I can't make it to dinner tonight, but I can swing by afterwards. Although I don't know what time that will be." He'd really wanted to take Ileana home to bed later if dinner went well. He kissed that chance good-bye.

"I'm glad we'll see you later. Your father and I need to discuss something with you."

Michael sat straighter in his chair, every nerve in his body screaming a warning. "About what?"

"We'll discuss it tonight. I know you're busy."

"Mom, tell me," he ordered.

There was a brief silence, then, "The doctor ordered some blood tests because I've been feeling tired."

His mom had taught school right up to her mastectomy. If she was admitting to tiredness, she must be exhausted. "When will you have the results?" His voice sounded like broken glass.

"In a few days."

His breath whooshed out. "Did Dr. Ramos make any guesses? Is the cancer back?"

"He said to wait for the results."

"If it's cancer, we need to act fast."

"I know, honey. That's what your father and I want to talk to you about."

"I think we should tell Charlie too."

"No." Her tone was that of the schoolteacher to a disruptive student. "I won't spoil his day."

Michael's hand fisted in frustration. "What about Rick?"

"Analise isn't feeling well. It's too hot for her to be working outside when she's seven months pregnant, so Rick is running her company in the evenings."

"I didn't know cemeteries were open after dark."

"He got special permission from most of the ones in Dade County because of her condition. I'm sure it helped that he's a policeman."

"That doesn't mean he knows how to take care of graves or plant flowers."

"Analise tells him what to do."

Damn it, it was time his brothers shared some of this burden. Why did it all fall on *his* shoulders? "I'll be there tonight. You can count on me." As usual. It sucked being the oldest child.

"I know we can, honey. I love you for it."

"I love you too, Mom. See you later." Michael disconnected before he could get choked up.

Damn it, not the cancer again. What good was all his growing wealth if it couldn't stop his mom from getting sick? He hadn't been able to stop his brother Billy from dying. What if...? He ruthlessly squelched that thought.

Something snapped. He looked down to see his mechanical pencil now in two pieces in his hand. He already paid for his mom to see the best oncologist in Miami. Should he fly in the country's top doctors if the tests came back positive for cancer? Hell, he could afford it. That's what he was making money for.

Determined, he called up his inventory on his laptop. He had to sell everything they'd imported and at a profit. If his mom needed an experimental treatment anywhere in the world, or anything else to make her well, he'd get it. And if someone was stealing from one of his warehouses, that person had better beware. Michael needed all the profit he could get to protect his mom.

CHAPTER 2

It took the entire drive back to the Calderon Consortium to cool Ileana's hormones and that was with the air conditioner blowing full blast. She hadn't felt this aware of a man since her *novio* Roberto. She didn't know how she was going to have a reasonable conversation with Michael Ziffkin over dinner when all she could think about was his hands on her breasts and then his mouth.

She groaned. How could she face her father all flushed like this? He'd know something was going on. She'd have to avoid him for a little while, at least until she got her body under control.

The large warehouse that housed her family's offices had been the locus of the Calderon Consortium for nearly forty years. Her family should have moved into the new millennium by finding a more modern building, but this one was the heart and soul of their company. She was the third generation of Calderon in the company, the first to be born an American citizen. This building and what it represented was why her grandparents had fled Cuba in 1961. In America, they'd found a future.

Ileana patted the wooden building with affection as she pulled open the door. Two stories of offices greeted her, as well as her young cousin Carona, manning the reception desk.

"How did the meeting go?" Carona asked. She was eighteen and engaged to be married. She'd leave the company as soon as she was wed.

"Very well. Some very nice things have come in from overseas. I predict a good sales year for us." Ileana continued past reception as she answered.

"That's good to hear. Very good."

Ileana strode down the left corridor to her small, cramped office. Calderon did not waste money on overhead, so she was used to her family's close proximity.

Unfolding the copy of the order Michael had printed, Ileana studied the list. Some of the items were a break from tradition. She'd have to justify the gamble to her father. But she felt tourists would buy them. Stock had gotten a little old-fashioned, she'd thought. It was time to update. But a risk to Calderon was a risk to the family.

A part of Ileana wished she could tell her father she'd seen this move in one of her dreams. He'd bluster, but he wouldn't argue. But she never lied about her dreams. That would be worse than sinful.

By avoiding thoughts of Michael, Ileana eventually felt calm enough to mount the stairs to the second floor to face her father. He had the biggest office on the second floor with windows in the front to look out over reception, and a glass wall in the back that overlooked the warehouse. It also had a private staircase down to the warehouse below.

Her father saw her through the windows and waved her in. He'd grown thicker in the past decade, and his black hair was liberally salted with gray. He'd turned sixty last month, too young to have to step down from the presidency. But having many younger family relations to do his legwork combined with his love of good food had conspired to unseat him.

She studied his face as she walked around his desk. His cheeks were florid, a sign of high blood pressure. She wondered whether he'd followed the doctor's diet at breakfast.

"How did your first buying trip go, Ileana?" He spoke in Spanish, as he usually did with her.

Ileana handed him the order. "It went well, Papá."

He scanned the piece of paper, his stout finger running down the items. His still-black brows crimped together. Finally, he looked up at her, his dark eyes intent.

"What is this? There are items on here we do not usually buy. I thought you knew what we sell in our stores."

Ileana took in a breath. "I do know, Papá. I also know what our competition is selling and they're carrying more modern merchandise. They're selling it too. We need to update. We need cell phone covers, ear buds, chargers, and jump drives, just to name a few."

"We have grown every year since my papá started Calderon. We must be doing something right. There is no reason to change."

"Papá, the tourists shopping in our stores aren't Cubans. They're Americans, modern ones. They have cell phones, iPads and MP3 players. They have DVD players in their SUVs. If they don't find what fits their lifestyle in our stores, they're going to spend their money at our competitors."

"Modern, *pah*. Modern does not mean better. Look at how you speak to me, with your modern ways."

"I'm not disrespecting you, Papá. This is business. Smart business."

"I am the papá. I am supposed to tell you what to do. A dutiful daughter would obey me."

"I am dutiful. I work every day for Calderon."

"You should be married and taking care of your husband and your children and your household, not Calderon."

Ileana pulled herself to her full height, towering over her father. "Roberto is dead. My chance of having a husband and children died with him. But he loved Calderon. He would want me to carry on in his place."

Her father took hold of her hands. "*Niña*, you did not die with Roberto. There are other good Cuban men you could marry. Your brother has many friends, respected doctors like him. Juan Carlos and your cousins know many eligible young men." Excitement laced her father's next words. "The Hernandez heir has finished his period of mourning for his wife. His father and I have talked about a merger. A blood tie would seal the deal."

Ileana slipped her hands free. "Hernandez is fifteen years older than me and has three teenage daughters."

"He can give you children of your own, Ileana. It is time, past time, for you to marry. I have put off this task long enough, giving you time, respecting your grief over Roberto. But your grief is excessive. If not Hernandez, then what of the other merchant families: Gutierrez, Reyes, Suarez—all good Cuban families. Calderon would do well to merge with any of them."

"Papá, I have met no one who moves me the way Roberto did." If she didn't count Michael Ziffkin.

"My precious daughter," her father's eyes were warm with love. "Perhaps a lesser love would do for you. You and Roberto—I have never seen two more suited people than you two. But you could find another Cuban man who shares similar interests, and you could build a good life with him."

"I want what you and Mamá have." The flame of love between her parents was strong.

"Love can grow, *chica*. You must give it a chance."

She gritted her teeth in frustration. She did not want a cold marriage to a stranger and have to allow him to touch her as Roberto had. The thought of what she and Michael had done in her dream heated her cheeks. She still felt the resonance of his forceful intrusion between her thighs and inside her body. Flames of passion had consumed them both. It had been no cold claiming, but an inferno of desire. Even if she fought it because it was wrong, how could she tie herself to her own kind knowing she could not share what she had with Michael?

And yet she owed a duty to her family.

"Juan Carlos's wife is with child," her father added. "He has done his duty to his family. If he were to become president of Calderon, he would have an heir for the company."

For a moment, despair washed over her. Her cousin would win the presidency. Then she straightened her spine. "I know my duty, Papá."

"Good. Very good. These new items," he waved the order form, "We will watch to see how well they sell."

"They'll do well. You'll see."

Ileana escaped to her office. She'd met no man in her circle of acquaintances that interested her enough to accept a date. Her mind strayed to Michael and tonight's dinner, which was not a date. Had she been as modern as she portrayed herself to her father, she'd have accepted Michael's invitation, knowing full well that she would go home with him afterwards. But she wasn't nearly as modern as she wanted to be. Even if she were, Michael wasn't Cuban.

Hours later as she collected her purse to leave, her desk phone rang.

"I have wonderful news," her mother exclaimed. "Caridad is pregnant."

Her *youngest* sister. Ileana forced a smile. "That's wonderful, Mamá. I know she's wanted a baby for awhile."

"I am a lucky woman to be blessed with another grandchild. Do you not agree?"

"Yes, Mamá."

"Even your brother Federico, as busy as he is with his medical practice, has given me a beautiful grandson. Little Fico was here today. Does my news not make you want a little one of your own, *niña*?"

"Yes, it does." But her brother had a wife, whereas Ileana had no husband. She'd been robbed of the chance to have one. "Mamá, you know why I have no children."

"It is time you turned away from Roberto's grave and began to live again. There are many good Cuban men who would gladly give you children and a home. You are a little old, but you still have your looks."

"I have a home already, Mamá."

"There is no man there. It is not truly a home until you share it with a man."

Ileana despaired of ever teaching her Cuban parents that there were more options for a woman than getting married and having children. Although that had been her dream, too, when Roberto was alive, she'd grown beyond that now.

"Mamá, I have a business meeting I have to go to. I'll call Caridad tonight and congratulate her."

"Business, *niña*, after hours?" Her mother sounded horrified.

"Yes, Mamá. I'll talk to you tomorrow." Gently Ileana hung up the phone.

She loved her family. They were the foundation of her life. They'd kept her going after Roberto died, when all she'd wanted to do was lie down next to him in his grave and make the pain stop. But they thought they owned her body and soul. She'd tear herself in half trying to prove they didn't.

CHAPTER 3

Ileana arrived at The Wharf Restaurant early, hoping for time to compose herself before she met Michael again. But he was the first person she saw as her eyes adjusted to the dim interior. As he paced towards her, her lungs seized and her pulse threatened to gallop out of control. He wore the jacket to his navy suit and looked delectable.

"Hi." His smooth voice welcomed her. His warm brown eyes appraised and approved.

She had to swallow to unlock her throat. "Hi."

He was near enough for her to smell his clean scent, to feel the warmth of his body invade her tight muscles and begin a melting sensation inside. Surely he could hear her heart pound. Ileana wanted badly to be pressed against his flesh.

"You look beautiful in that dress."

"Thank you." Darn, she felt flustered. She shouldn't have changed clothes. This wasn't a date. He would get the wrong idea.

"Navy suits you." The words slipped out of her mouth, and she was horrified he might guess her wanton thoughts.

"Your table is ready, Mr. Ziffkin."

Ileana hadn't seen the hostess approach. In fact, she hadn't noticed anything but Michael since she'd set foot in the door. Her face burned.

She was preternaturally aware of Michael's warm hand at her waist as he guided her to their table. As he seated her, she brushed against him, and her nerve endings went haywire.

How was she going to hold an intelligent conversation with him? She was grateful for a few moments' respite as the waitress appeared and took their drink orders. Ileana sipped her water to moisten her dry mouth. The Wharf was a mid-range restaurant, a little pricey for families, so the atmosphere was hushed, yet not ostentatious.

Ileana watched Michael drink his water and her mouth dried all over again. She could imagine his lips on hers, consuming her with kisses until they were out of breath. His long fingers circled the slender glass stem. She pictured it full of wine and him tilting it over her naked body. Then he'd follow the liquid down to sip at her flesh with those same lips. Her nipples pebbled painfully with yearning.

"Do you know what you want?" he asked.

You. It was a cry from her painfully awakened body. She'd been encased in ice for more than a decade and it hurt to thaw. She ached wanting what she should not have.

Michael stared at her, and awareness pulsed between them. She shouldn't have come. The risk was too high being this near him.

"Yes, I know what I want." Was that husky-sounding siren her?

"Good." His voice sounded thick.

Had his eyes darkened, or was it just the intimate lighting? She'd thought his choice of restaurant perfect for a business meeting. She hadn't counted on the understated elegance, the hush caused by the thick carpeting, or the lighted candle on their table which tricked her mind into thinking of romance.

This is business, she scolded herself sternly.

When the waitress brought their drinks, they ordered, and the young woman left them alone.

"How big is Citadel?"

"So your parents' parents started Calderon."

They spoke at the same time. Michael waved with his hand. "Ladies first."

"I wondered how big your company is."

"I grossed $4.5 million last year. I have four warehouses now and a corporate office, although I'm the only corporate officer."

"I told Papá we needed a corporate office, but he said Calderon began where it is and should stay there."

"Where your grandparents started the business?"

She nodded. "Yes, nearly fifty years ago. Yet they still talk about going back to the old country—to Cuba. I think they're hoping to outlive Castro."

"He doesn't show signs of dying anytime soon."

"I know. But it's their dream and shared by most Cubans in Miami including my parents. People talk about it all the time in Little Havana."

"Is it your dream, Ileana?"

"No," she denied with fervor. "I was born an American. This is my home, not Cuba. I don't want to live there."

"So if somehow your parents and grandparents returned to Cuba, you'd stay here?"

Ileana wanted to agree immediately, but she'd never thought about being separated from her relatives by ninety miles of ocean. Moving to her own place didn't really count as being separated from them.

Slowly she answered him. "Yes, I'd stay here. But it would be hard not having them nearby. We're a very close family."

"How big is your family?"

"I have three sisters, my brother who's a doctor, and their spouses and children. All live within a few miles of my parents and grandparents. I talk to at least one of them every day. My aunts, uncles, and cousins also live close by and are a regular part of our lives. Most of them live in or around Little Havana."

Ileana didn't know how they'd strayed so far from business, but suddenly she was curious about Michael Ziffkin the man. "What about your family? Do they live here? Do you have brothers and sisters?"

Michael had been leaning towards her with his arms on the table. Now he sat back and crossed his arms across his chest. His face smoothed into the serious look she'd seen earlier today. "My parents and two brothers live here. My younger brother Rick is married, and his first child is due in two months. My youngest brother Charlie is getting married in less than two weeks."

He talked about them almost as if they were strangers. His manner was stiff, inviting no comment. Ileana wanted badly to ask what was wrong, whether he didn't like his family and why, but Michael's eyes had lost their warmth. Her heart ached to comfort him, her arms yearned to hold him, but he was a stranger.

Luckily, the waitress chose that moment to slide their entrees in front of them, and for a few moments, they ate in silence.

"How long until your father retires?" Michael asked.

He was all business, and Ileana tried to match his tone. "A few months maybe, no later than the end of the year."

"Can I assume you've worked in the company for years?"

She smiled. "Nearly all my life. It's a family business after all."

"And your distant cousin who's vying for the presidency, he's worked there all his life, too?"

Ileana refused to talk trash about family. "Nearly."

"Who do you think is the better candidate, you or him?"

She ducked her head as her face heated. Her modern, American half vied with her traditional Cuban half. The American in her won. "I believe I am. I understand the market beyond Cuban and Hispanic wants. I spent four years at Florida State immersing myself in cultures not my own. I pay attention to what's going on outside Little Havana, so I know more about American tourists."

"Your cousin doesn't understand the market?"

She demurred. "Juan Carlos is more...traditional. He will continue to purchase as my father purchased and from the same vendors. You should not fear having him as president."

Michael's dark gaze sharpened. "You would change vendors?"

"I liked what I saw today." That was an understatement. And immediately, her clothes felt too tight again. She went on quickly.

"I liked the new items I bought. I'd like to try even more new things." Oh, she was getting in even deeper without trying.

The warmth in his eyes said he agreed.

The meal continued without incident. Ileana was aware of his presence like the sun on her skin. She felt flushed. His ardent perusal made her pulse take flight again and again.

She watched his lips and strong white teeth as he chewed his broiled snapper. She watched his Adam's apple bob as he swallowed. His fingers were long and sure, confident when handling his silverware. She liked the play of candlelight on the planes of his face, in the darkness of his hair.

Her crab-stuffed flounder was delicious. The explosion of taste on her tongue only whet her appetite for the dessert sitting across from her.

What would it be like to feed morsels to one another and then share kisses between bites? To share while sitting in his lap? To share while they were naked, after lovemaking. And partway through the meal, Michael would ease her down onto his hardening length. In that position, they could tease one another while they finished nibbling. When their plates were empty—maybe before—they would nibble on each other. A torrid lovemaking session would follow to sate all their appetites.

Ileana fanned herself. Her blush burned her cheeks. She hadn't had such carnal thoughts in years. She wished with all her might that she was as modern as she'd told Michael she was. Then she'd go home with him tonight—or take him home—and neither of them would get any sleep as she fed her hunger for him.

"You're staring." Again, Michael's voice was husky.

Ileana licked her lips. She couldn't tell him she found him sexy and attractive and wanted to strip him naked so she could have her way with him, and vice versa.

Instead, she dropped her gaze and said, "I don't mean to."

"I don't mind."

Her gaze snapped back up. "You don't?"

"No, not at all."

His smile made something melt in her lower abdomen. Her return smile was just as approving of his sexiness.

"Ileana, I know you wanted this to be a business dinner, but..." A soft buzzing interrupted him. He frowned. "Please excuse me. I'll just see if this is the call I'm waiting for."

Michael pulled his black cell phone from his suit jacket and glanced at the read-out. His frown deepened and he answered it. "This is Ziffkin."

As he listened, his expression darkened. "No, you did the right thing. Have you called the police? Good. I'll be there in about twenty-five minutes."

He replaced his phone and true regret played in his eyes. "There's been a break-in. I have to go."

On impulse, Ileana offered, "I'll go with you."

His features grew grim. "No. Please stay and finish your dinner." He signaled the waitress over as he rose. "There's an emergency. I have to leave. If Miss Alvarez Calderon wants anything more..."

Ileana rose, too. "I'm finished."

"Then I need the bill immediately."

"Certainly, sir. If you'll follow me, I'll get you cashed out."

In moments, they stood in the lighted parking lot. Fate had intervened to prevent Ileana from doing something foolhardy. Had Michael not received that call, she would have gladly accepted a kiss, which she knew would have soon gotten out of control.

Michael stood in front of her with the same awareness in his eyes, but he rocked on his heels, anxious to leave.

In the awkwardness, Ileana fell into the habit of familiar manners. "Thank you for dinner, but you shouldn't have paid. The next time will be on me."

"I wish I had more time."

"I understand. I won't keep you."

Michael hesitated a moment more, then visibly tore himself from her presence. He strode to the other side of the parking lot.

Ileana watched him go, strangely feeling let-down, as though she'd missed something important.

CHAPTER 4

Michael hated leaving Ileana. Except for a few awkward moments when she'd brought up his family, they'd got on like a house on fire. His burning erection was a testament to that. And the way she'd looked at him—like she wanted to eat him up—had made his blood head south in a hurry.

Now, damn it, instead of heading home with her to see how many ways they could indulge their mutual lust, he had to return to business.

His gut twisted. A break-in, his security guard had said. Is that how inventory had gone missing at his other warehouse?

Traffic made him want to yell with frustration and rage. He needed to get there. Who knew how long he'd be tied up with the cops. Damn it...his parents. At the next red light he pulled out his cell phone and rang them. His dad answered.

"Dad, an emergency came up at one of my warehouses. I'm going to be tied up for several more hours. I can still come over tonight, but it might be late."

"Son," he could hear his dad moving then he spoke more quietly, "You aren't avoiding your brother, are you?"

Guilt momentarily ate at him, and then anger pushed it back. "No, I'm not. Someone broke into my warehouse. I'm headed there now to meet the police."

"Oh, I'm sorry to hear that." His father paused. "It's just something your mother said."

"Dad, I'm doing the best I can to help you and Mom, so you won't have to worry about anything. That means I don't have a lot of free time."

"We don't expect you to pay for everything, Michael. We never asked for that."

"You took care of me when I was young. I owe you for that. I want to help."

"But if helping us means you don't have time for your brothers..."

"Dad, they're both young and in love. They don't want their big brother in the way."

"Is it because they found someone special and you haven't? Michael, there's someone out there if you'd just look."

Michael's thoughts flew to Ileana. She made him feel things he hadn't felt in...well, he couldn't remember ever feeling that hot about a woman before. But he would not marry. He couldn't risk his heart like that. He'd already lost one family member when his brother died.

"I'll call you as soon as I'm finished, unless it's after eleven. I know Mom needs her rest."

"It's important that we talk to you soon."

"I know. I'll call you."

Frustrated rage seethed through Michael at so many urgent conflicting demands on his limited time—his parents foremost. He needed his mom to receive a clean bill of health from the doctor. He had to stop whoever was stealing from him. That was profit he might use to pay for his mom's treatment. And he wanted to see Ileana again.

He couldn't just call her and invite her to his house for some satisfying sex. She required a lead-in, like dinner had been tonight. She needed seduction in order to let her guard down. He wondered if it was her Cuban upbringing.

Michael cursed the thieves for stealing his time with Ileana. He'd have to try to coax her into a date, even though she'd made her views on dating clear.

But her eyes had sent a different message at dinner.

Finally he pulled up to the warehouse. A police car sat in the street outside. Good, he wouldn't have to wait for them. He pushed through the side door and was greeted by his security guard and two police officers: one African-American and one Hispanic.

"I'm sorry, sir…" the Latino cop began.

"Mr. Ziffkin," Michael's security guard overrode the cop. "I was just telling these officers what I found. These are officers Hernandez and Forster."

"You're the owner?" The cop's nametag identified him as Hernandez.

"Yes. Harry, do you know if anything was stolen?" Michael asked the guard.

Harry Gardino was fifty-seven and a former marine who still wore his black hair in a crew cut. "I haven't had a chance to look at the merchandise yet. As soon as I found the open door I checked the premises for intruders but found none. Then I called you."

"Mr. Ziffkin, we'd like you to take a look," Officer Forster suggested, "and see if anything obvious is missing."

"Sure," Michael agreed.

The medium-sized warehouse held a lot of goods. Since he visited regularly, he knew the merchandise. He was a hands-on manager. Desiree would call him a control freak.

Whoever broke in had left the cheap trinkets alone as well as the medium-priced items. He didn't trade in a lot of the more expensive items because he sold mainly to tourist retail shops. But when he entered the section of the warehouse where the upscale items were stored, he saw the bare spots immediately.

"They went after the higher-end items. At least a couple of crates are missing." The more expensive items moved slower and were therefore kept towards the back of the warehouse. How much time had the thieves had to look through the place?

"Harry, how long between rounds?"

"It was two hours this time. I checked. And I vary my routine."

"They must have been casing the place," Hernandez surmised.

"How'd they know what to take?" Michael asked.

"Depends on how long they've been watching," Forster replied.

"A determined person could find a place to hide where he could track comings and goings and what gets unloaded," Hernandez added.

Michael wondered if the thieves were watching all his properties.

Harry seemed to wonder the same thing because he asked, "You want us to step up patrols, Mr. Ziffkin?"

"Yeah. I'll call your dispatcher and confirm it then talk to your office in the morning." Michael pulled out his cell phone and typed in those reminders. Then everyone moved towards the front of the warehouse.

"We'll try to lift fingerprints off the door, but we're assuming it sees a lot of traffic," Hernandez explained.

"Meaning it's unlikely to identify the thieves that way," Michael interpreted.

Hernandez nodded. "I'm sorry. That's reality."

"The burglary detectives will need a list of what was stolen," Forster added. "We have a better chance of catching them when they fence the goods."

Michael nodded.

A car pulled up outside the door. The cops stiffened as did Michael and Harry, but when two men in lightweight suits got out, the officers relaxed.

"That'll be the burglary detectives." Hernandez nodded to Michael. "You're in good hands."

It was a repeat of talking to the beat cops. After Harry gave his statement, he got into the security car to continue his patrol. The detectives fingerprinted the door and warned Michael again of the unlikelihood of useable prints.

They gave Michael their business cards and drove away, leaving him alone to wait for the locksmith. He checked his watch—it was ten-thirty. The locksmith had several emergency jobs ahead of Michael's, and had projected a two-hour wait.

Michael moved his Mazda 626 directly in front of the warehouse door. He didn't think the thieves would return tonight, but if they did, they'd have to go through him. All he had to armor himself against the criminal element was his anger, which at this point still had his adrenalin pumping hard. He could do some serious damage with a bat. He broke off a piece of wood from a pallet. It gave a satisfying *thunk* against his palm.

Removing his suit jacket, he rolled one of the office chairs out to the entrance and sat inside the door. Someone had already targeted two of his warehouses. He couldn't swear the two events were related, but his gut said they were. He was only one man. He couldn't guard all his properties simultaneously. He'd have to weigh the cost of additional security against what he'd lost so far. And tomorrow he'd have to pay his staff overtime or bring in an outside firm to do inventory. His insurance would cover the theft, but he had a deductible and had to worry about his premiums going up as a result.

Michael gripped the arms of the chair. He needed neither the added worry of the thefts, nor the expense involved right now. While his mom awaited her test results, he needed to be focused on her and contingency plans for her care, if the news was bad.

He needed to call his parents. They shouldn't have to wait if they needed to discuss something important with him. Damn it, why hadn't he knocked off work early to see them? Why had he chosen to have dinner with Ileana instead? Since when did his needs come before theirs? Realization hit with the force of a fist. If the break-in hadn't happened, he would have gone home with Ileana for some hot sex and maybe blown off his parents. How selfish did that make him? Now was no time to have an affair. He wasn't some lust-blinded animal who couldn't keep his priorities straight when a hot babe walked by.

Michael pulled his cell phone out of his pocket and dialed his parents. His dad answered again.

"I'm not going to make it over tonight, Dad. I'm waiting for the locksmith and he's got a two-hour backlog."

His dad sighed. "It's all right. When I saw the time, I realized you probably weren't going to make it."

"I'm sorry. I know my timing sucks."

His dad snorted. "I can hardly blame you for a break-in. Did they take much?"

Michael sighed and rubbed his face. "As far as I can tell, they got a couple of crates of more expensive stuff. We have to do an inventory tomorrow to find out how much we lost."

"I'm sorry, son."

"I'm insured," he tried to reassure his dad. "Listen, how about if I come over on the way to work tomorrow?"

"Michael, you'll be lucky to get to bed by one o'clock. You don't need to try to squeeze us in before work."

"I don't mind, really."

"Why don't you just come over for dinner tomorrow night and we'll talk about it then?"

"I don't want Mom to have to cook for guests two nights in a row."

"I'm doing the cooking, son. Your mother makes the salad. What time can we expect you?"

Michael gave in. "Is six-thirty too late?"

"We'll see you then."

The warehouse was quiet with only him inside. Michael wished Ileana were here so they could talk. Talk, right. But he'd savored the moments with her today. They had a lot in common professionally. Right now he'd like to share what had happened. Ileana would understand. Most women wouldn't. He wouldn't even have to mention his parents.

He wished he could call Desiree and Jamal, but it was too late at night for that. Their son, Tyrell, would be asleep and the phone might wake him. Damn. How had he gotten to this point where there was no one he could call at ten-thirty at night to share his worries or even pass the time?

Michael retrieved his laptop from the trunk of his car, inserted his wireless card and did an Internet search for new cancer treatments. This was where he needed to focus. There was time to build friendships after his mom was well.

CHAPTER 5

Michael's mom looked tired when she answered the door. His gut twisted and his chest tightened with worry. He refused to think the cancer was back.

On impulse, he kissed her cheek. "Hi, Mom."

She looked him over with a keen gaze, despite the dark circles under her eyes. That look had pinned many a student to the wall until he or she confessed some wrongdoing. Michael and his brothers hadn't been exempt from that eye at home. He controlled an urge to fidget.

Then his mom shook her head. "Sorry, honey. I can't break my old habits. Your father told me about the break-in. Did they get much?"

Michael hooked his arm through hers as they walked towards the kitchen. She was a petite powerhouse of a woman, fifty-eight years old and trim. Her short dark hair had white in it now, new since it had grown back after the chemo.

"Not much. They seemed to want particular items, so I'm lucky they didn't take more."

"I'm sorry you missed Charlie and Juliana. I always liked her."

"Were you matchmaking even when they were kids?"

His mom struck his arm. "Don't be absurd. But there was something when they were together..."

"That was hormones, Mom. She looked hot in that Catholic school uniform. Even I wasn't immune."

"Don't let Charlie hear you talk about his fiancé like that."

"He heard me talk that way as a teenager. Heck, he said so himself."

"Well they're getting married in less than two weeks, so you'd better forget you ever had those thoughts." They entered the bright, gleaming kitchen. "Besides, this was when they were children. He was a better actor when she was around, and she had a habit of becoming totally absorbed by him. I wondered if they were meant to be together. But then the Sanchezes moved away, and I thought I'd been wrong."

She gave him a dazzling smile. "But I was right."

"You usually are." He waved to his dad through the sliding glass patio doors. "Dad's grilling." He hosted a hope for a thick, juicy burger.

Which crashed and burned at his mother's next words. "We're having swordfish steaks."

Cancer had changed his parents' lifestyle. They'd given up red meat, ate more fresh fruits and vegetables, and walked daily. Michael swallowed any complaints.

As his mom tossed the salad, he took a bottle of water out to his dad. Joe Ziffkin was a tall, wide-shouldered fifty-eight-year-old whose hair was still mostly dark. Michael shared his dark eyes. The lines around his dad's eyes were more pronounced since they'd begun the fight with cancer.

Michael handed his father the chilled water and they both sipped as the fish sizzled.

"Mom looks tired," Michael blurted.

"We'll talk about it after dinner." His father's stern look and tone shut Michael up. His gut tightened with fear. The news was bad if his dad didn't want to talk about it. He flailed for some innocuous subject.

"Mom says she knew Charlie and Juliana would be together."

His father looked towards the house and smiled indulgently. "Yes, she told me so. Rick surprised her with Analise though."

"He would." Rick, two years younger than Michael, had a restless streak. He'd amazed everyone by becoming a cop. That restlessness had taken him away from Miami, but now he was back home again and happily settled down with his wife, Analise.

"Your mother wouldn't mind being surprised by you," his father said.

Michael swung his gaze to his father's. Despite the light tone, his father's eyes were serious. Dread filled Michael. Was it just the maternal need to see her children married, or was it something more? He couldn't bring himself to even name it. He swallowed hard and looked away, not wanting his father to see his fear.

"You've never brought a woman home to meet us, Michael."

And he probably never would. He couldn't risk the pain of loving someone, of being responsible for them, and failing to protect them. Like Billy. Like his mom.

He forced a smile for his dad. "I'm only thirty-six. I've got plenty of time to get serious about someone."

"Your brothers are younger than you, and they've both found someone."

"Charlie's known Juliana since they were kids," Michael argued. He saw his mother signaling from the house and sighed with relief. The inquisition was over...for now.

Dinner was a slightly stilted affair. His parents told him all the wedding and baby news. Michael was glad his brothers' happy events had helped his mom through the last of her treatment.

While he'd carried the burden of the worries.

They cleared the table, loaded the dishwasher, and then his dad pulled out a chair for his mom. There was no putting off this talk. Michael took a seat across from them. His throat dried.

"We haven't heard from the doctor yet," his mother began.

Michael's breath whooshed out.

"But we thought we should be prepared, just in case," his father continued. "We need to update our wills..."

"Wills," Michael choked.

"They haven't been updated in twenty years," his father explained. "You kids were minors then. We've still got you going to a guardian."

"And William is in there," his mother said softly. "Our estate should be split between the three of you boys."

Michael couldn't discuss this with them, not staring at the lines deeply grooved in his mother's face. Not while looking at her new hair that was a different color and texture since it grew back. Not while he knew they were afraid of the test results.

"Nothing bad is going to happen to you." He said it to them as much as to himself.

"We think it's smart to be prepared," his mother said.

"Everybody's will should be up-to-date," his father nodded his head.

"Yes, I agree," Michael conceded.

His father took a deep breath. "We want to buy cemetery plots."

Michael couldn't breathe. For a moment a picture of his brother Billy's grave filled his mind. That small patch of ground meant despair and pain.

His mother smiled at him. "There are some nice spaces near William's grave..."

"No!" Michael shouted. He was on his feet, his breath heaving. "You're not going to die!" The words cracked through the room like a gunshot.

His mother paled. Her lower lip trembled. His father turned a fierce scowl at Michael. Michael feared he would shatter. He'd never mentioned death in connection with his mother. Maybe he was superstitious. But hearing the words echo made the truth come alive.

"I've got all the latest research. There's a new treatment begun in China that's being performed now in India with a high rate of success. I found a place in Mexico. Even if it is cancer, I know what we can do this time. But it's not cancer. It's not."

He was trying to convince someone—his parents, himself, a higher power, he didn't know whom.

"Michael, we're just planning ahead. We'll need plots someday," his mother said with irrefutable logic.

But Michael argued anyway. "Not that soon."

"Michael, sit down," his father ordered. "We're naming you executor in our wills."

Michael slumped into his chair, his face in his hands.

"You're the oldest, after all," his mother added.

Of course. It always came down to that. While his younger brothers talked about baby showers and honeymoons, he heard about prepaid funeral expenses, cremation versus burial, and organ donation. It got harder to breathe the longer his parents talked. His chest tightened painfully. He dropped his hands and simply stared at his parents.

Didn't they know what this talk of death was doing to him? Couldn't they see they were hurting him?

"No," he spoke into the silence. "I won't let you die."

"We're not planning to die," his father said. "We're planning for the future."

Michael shook his head. "You're thinking negatively. You can't do that. I've seen studies on the healing power of positive attitude. And you're using up Mom's energy on things that won't make her stronger."

His mother reached across the small glass table to touch his hand. "Michael, I'm doing everything I'm supposed to in order to recover. I need this for my peace of mind."

Michael rubbed a shaking hand across his forehead, wiping away cold sweat. It was just a superstition, but he couldn't shake it. He dare not voice it aloud either, lest that give it substance as well.

If they bought cemetery plots, they might need them.

His dad gripped his mom's hand. "We don't need your permission, Michael. But we'd like your support."

Michael couldn't condemn them to death. A cold hand touched him at the thought, making him shudder.

"Mom, Dad, I've been here for you since Billy died. I've been with you every step of the way as you fought the cancer. If you needed anything to regain your health, I'd move heaven and earth to get it for you. I'd sell my company. Hell, I'd sell my condo and live here with you. I'd fly you anywhere in the world to get you any treatment. But I can't watch you pick out your graves. I just can't. If you think that means I don't love you enough, I'm sorry I disappointed you." He rose from his seat.

"Michael," his mother objected sharply.

"Son, we thought nothing of the sort."

Then Michael felt guilty. "I'd give my life for both of you." He headed for the front door before he cracked.

His father's firm hand on his shoulder stopped him before he could leave. "We've put a burden on you a son shouldn't have to bear."

"I don't mind."

"I know you don't. We've grown to count on you."

Michael turned to see his parents' serious faces. "I know." He hugged his dad hard and then his mom. "I love you."

And then he fled.

CHAPTER 6

"One of our stores was robbed last night," Esteban Calderon reported to his heirs. "And one of the Hernandez stores was hit last week."

"Citadel Import-Export had a break-in two nights ago," Ileana remembered. "Could these robberies be related?"

Juan Carlos gave her a sharp look. "How do you know that?"

"I've been getting to know our suppliers. I was having dinner with Michael Ziffkin when he got the call about the break-in."

"Dinner, Ileana?" Her father's voice was sharp.

"A business dinner, Papá. You have those."

"Not with an unmarried man. Not without your family to escort you."

"Papá, I'm twenty-nine years old. I don't need a chaperon at a business dinner."

"Juan Carlos could have gone in your place."

"I'm meeting suppliers, Papá, as a representative of Calderon. Because I'm a woman doesn't mean I'm meeting prospective husbands."

"Ileana," her father reprimanded. "Show a little more respect. Of course Ziffkin is not a prospective husband. He is white."

They'd gotten away from the topic. Ileana steered it back. "What have you found out about the robberies?"

"I have found nothing. I want the two of you to solve them and prevent any more thefts."

"Isn't that the police's job?" Ileana asked.

"The police offer no hope. They do not know the Hernandez robbery might be related to ours. But the two of you do. Start there. Ileana, go and talk to Hernandez. Remember that Calderon is the oldest of the family-owned chains. The others look to us to lead."

When Ileana and Juan Carlos left her father's office, she took the reins. "We should divide the list of chains and contact all of them."

"I'll make the list. I'll put it on your desk when I'm finished so you can make your calls when you get back."

"It will take less time to call Hernandez."

"*Tio* Esteban wants you to go there in person. I agree with him."

"You were Roberto's brother. How can you push me towards Hernandez?"

"Roberto is dead, Ileana. Long dead. You are not. I understand how his death was a terrible blow for a sensitive seventeen-year-old girl, but my brother would not have wanted you to remain unmarried for his sake. *Tio* Esteban wants a merger between the families. I want a merger. You say you want what's best for the family, for Calderon. Then do your duty. The head of Calderon works for the good of all of us."

Ileana bit back a scathing retort as he retreated to his office. Juan Carlos had done his duty for his family and hers. He'd stepped into Roberto's shoes at Calderon, married a daughter of a Cuban family owning a chain of restaurants, and would soon produce an heir. Juan Carlos may not have solidified the merchant families, but he'd cemented a link with another line of Cuban exiles. It was about tying the Cuban community together.

That he'd made a love match in the bargain was amazing. It also made Ileana angry that he wanted her to settle for less, especially after he'd seen what she'd shared with his brother.

Ileana tracked down Emilio Hernandez, heir and acting president of the Hernandez family chain of retail shops, in the middle of his monthly inspection tour. He agreed to meet her in an hour at one of his shops on the beachfront.

Emilio greeted her with a kiss on each cheek and a spark in his brown eyes that made Ileana's stomach hurt. He was a fit forty-five-year-old with jet-black hair and swarthy skin. He would be considered handsome...by a woman his age, or by a twenty-year-old whose family wanted a merger. Unfortunately, Ileana fell in the middle—too young to be impressed and too old to be naïve.

"It is so good to see you again, Ileana. Your father is well?" Emilio's accent was almost as thick as her father's.

"As well as can be expected with his doctor telling him what to do."

"Yes, he is a man who directs, not one who listens well."

He didn't have to tell her. "Your daughters are well?"

"They are a beautiful handful. They need a mother's love and guidance. Arletta will have her *quince* this year. It would be wonderful if she had a woman to talk to and guide her, one who understood how to choose a proper *novio*."

Ileana had met her *novio* at her *quince*, her fifteenth birthday party. But she was not prepared to take on ready-made motherhood or talk to any young girl about dating and marriage. After all, what did she know of marriage?

Emilio took hold of her hand. His was warm and dry. "My father has spoken to your father. I assume by your presence you are aware I have finished my period of mourning. You have finished yours. Our fathers would be pleased and delighted were I to become your *novio,* and after a proper period of courting, your husband. I need sons, Ileana." He stroked her palm.

Emilio's old-world Cuban manners reminded her of her father and grandfather. Those two men would, indeed, be delighted with Emilio's suggestion. Her mother and grandmothers would immediately begin to plan the wedding. She wouldn't even have to lift a finger. One day—no, one hour—after Emilio became her *novio* the Calderon and Hernandez lawyers would begin to iron out the merger details, which would await only the end of the nuptials to be signed.

One word from her would make dozens of people happy.

"You are a beautiful woman, Ileana."

But she wouldn't be one of them. She couldn't picture herself sharing physical intimacy with Emilio. A scene with Michael burst into her mind, of them doing the things she'd done with Roberto and more, other things she hadn't known to do because she'd been young and sheltered.

Well she wasn't sheltered now, or young. But she was a Calderon. "I'm flattered, Emilio, that you would trust me with your young daughters."

Emilio's face lit.

"But it's not true. I haven't finished my mourning for Roberto yet."

"But it has been so long. Perhaps I could help you to put your grief aside. Maybe you cannot do it alone. I have experience in this. You could trust me. I would be a gentle *novio*."

Duty beat at her. Her father's words, her mother's, Juan Carlos's. But she couldn't do it. "I know you would be gentle, but I'm not ready. I can't be what you need."

A frown marred his face, nearly anger, but he was Cuban enough not to show it to a marriageable female. "Then why are you here?"

"We had a break-in. My father said you did, too. We need to know if this was the same person or persons."

They sat at a small table in the back room and compared notes. Each store had been breached during the night via a hole cut in a window pane. A delivery had been made during the previous day. Emilio's stores stretched further south than theirs did. He'd heard of a break-in last week down the coast at a chain run by a Middle Eastern family.

"You think these break-ins are related," Emilio mused.

"Citadel Import-Export was robbed, too. We're all in the same business. It's too coincidental not to be related."

"It will be expensive to hire full-time security to protect our stores," he calculated.

"For us as well."

"But if it prevents further losses, I'll have to do it."

"Juan Carlos and I are looking into the matter. We'll do our best to stop these robberies so the families are safe."

Emilio nodded. "It is right that Calderon lead the way. But you need not stand alone, Ileana. A cousin is a strong right hand, but a husband could take your burdens from you and make the families strong in solidarity."

"I'll keep your offer in mind, Emilio." She rose.

Good manners had Emilio on his feet in an instant. He took her hands in his and brushed his lips against both her cheeks. His touch lingered longer than was proper. She knew he coveted her as his next wife. If only she could.

Ileana pulled gently away so as not to offer offense. "Thank you for meeting me, Emilio. I'll keep in touch."

He gave her a business card. "Here is my cell phone number. Feel free to call me."

"I will."

Ileana hurried to her car. She cursed her heritage and her family for putting her in this position where she felt guilty for wanting to live her own life, for wanting a man who loved her as the other half of his soul, and for wanting to stand by a man's side and deal with the dark side of life together as partners. She'd always accepted that a Cuban man was her destiny. But the longer she'd stayed single, the more she wanted from her marriage. She didn't want to be cosseted and relegated to child-rearing. She wanted to help her family's business grow and flourish. She'd seen beyond the Cuban stereotype. Why couldn't her family?

Michael's chest constricted. "How bad?"

"They ordered tests. Dr. Ramos wants us at the hospital this afternoon."

God, this couldn't be happening. Michael closed his eyes.

"He's going to meet us there and read the results himself," his father continued. "Michael," his father's voice broke. "Michael, she's all I have."

Michael's throat closed. His dad was losing it. "Nothing's going to happen to her, Dad. We'll take her to whatever specialists she needs in whatever country has a cure. We can beat this thing."

"That's what they said last time. They said we'd beaten it. They said we'd won, that she was clear. It's been months." His father drew a ragged breath. "She can't see me like this. I don't know how brave I can be today."

"Dad, I'll be there. What time do you have to be at the hospital?"

"Two o'clock, but you've got work to do. I don't expect you to have to hold my hand."

"I'll pick you and Mom up at one-thirty."

"But…"

"I want to do this, Dad."

His dad's sigh sounded relieved. "Thanks, son. I knew I could count on you."

"Where's Mom?"

"She's in the garden. I don't think she wanted me to see her cry." He choked.

Damn it. Michael rubbed at his face. He felt like crying himself or hurling something at the wall. "We'll beat this, Dad." His voice was hoarse.

"I'm sorry to fall apart like this."

"It's a shock. Don't let Mom see you. Tell her I'll be there in a few hours."

"Sure, son. We'll be waiting."

Michael ended the call and rubbed his forehead. His thoughts fragmented, racing a million miles an hour through every possibility. With difficulty, he reined them to a stop. Dr. Ramos would tell them what they needed to do.

"Michael?"

Slowly he looked up. He'd forgotten Ileana was there. Her beauty smote him once more, but not even lust could rise from the ashes of hope.

She rose and moved around his desk to face him unobstructed. "What is it?"

She was a stranger, a business associate. Except for Desiree, his co-workers knew very little about him personally, and he liked it that way. There was sympathy and concern on her lovely face. He'd carried the load alone for so long. He'd really like some of that caring aimed at him.

"My mom's cancer is back. We have to go to the hospital today to find out where it's spread." He would not break down in front of Ileana.

"How terrible for her and for you. I'm sorry. Is there anything I can do?"

Hold me. He trapped the vulnerable words behind his teeth, simply shaking his head. He'd been strong for his parents since his brother was murdered, had been there for them, been with them through the first cancer diagnosis. He'd be their support through this recurrence. That was his duty as the oldest son.

It had been his job as the oldest to protect Billy, too. But Billy was an adult. It was his right to move away from home, just as Rick and Charlie had done, and nothing had happened to either of them. But three times had not been the charm, and Billy had died.

Michael wouldn't let that happen to his mom. "Thanks for offering to help. It's very kind of you. But I'll make sure my parents have everything they need."

CHAPTER 7

"We'll need to remove the other breast," Dr. Ramos informed Michael and his parents.

Michael's mother's gasp sounded like pain. He squeezed her hand trying to imbue his strength into her. His father held her other hand in a white-knuckled grip. Her face was white and strained, the skin taut across her cheekbones.

"We'll take the lymph nodes, too, this time." Ernesto Ramos was the foremost oncologist in Miami. His black hair was touched with gray in a way that made him look handsome and distinguished.

"Her lungs?" Mr. Ziffkin's voice sounded hoarse.

"Clear," Dr. Ramos answered immediately and with evident relief. "I saw no other signs of cancer."

Mrs. Ziffkin sagged, her eyes closing.

"Did you miss something the first time?" Michael asked. "Is that why the cancer came back?"

"No, it's simply an aggressive cancer." Dr. Ramos held up his hand to forestall Michael's questions. "We've caught it very early, so with equally aggressive treatment we'll stop it."

"Chemo and radiation again?" Michael asked without looking at his mother.

"To be certain, yes."

Michael's mother made a little sound in her throat. Her hair had finally grown back out in time for Charlie's wedding, and she'd been getting ready to teach school again. He knew how sick the chemo made her, and he hated that she had to go through the ordeal again.

Michael grasped at one last straw. "Did you look over the information on the trials they're holding in India that I sent you?"

"I did, Michael. I believe the treatment plan I'll outline will be satisfactory. You and your parents won't have to leave the country." He turned to address Michael's mother. "Jane, I'd like to schedule surgery as soon as possible. How does Monday morning sound?"

She gave his father an agonized look then turned back to Dr. Ramos and lifted her chin. "My youngest son is getting married next weekend. I want to be at the wedding."

"Mom, Dr. Ramos thinks you need the surgery right away," Michael protested.

She shot him her schoolteacher glare, and he fought to keep from cringing. Her health was too important.

"I've waited so long for you boys to get married. Rick went down to the courthouse to marry Analise. This is the first real wedding one of my sons has had. I don't intend to miss it."

"Will a week make a difference, Dr. Ramos?" his father asked.

"No, a week won't make a difference. Shall we schedule the surgery for the Monday after next?"

Mrs. Ziffkin's eyes filled with tears. "Yes. That will work perfectly."

"The wedding will do wonders for your morale, I think," Dr. Ramos stated as he filled out paperwork.

"Yes it will. My son and his fiancé grew up together. Fate brought them together again."

Dr. Ramos cocked an eyebrow. "How strange to hear someone so down-to-earth say such a thing."

Michael's mom gave a small smile. "It's been a strange year."

Michael couldn't stand not knowing a minute longer. "What's the prognosis, Dr. Ramos?" He sensed the chill that overtook his parents.

Again, Dr. Ramos spoke to Mrs. Ziffkin. "I believe your prognosis is excellent. Between the surgery, the chemo, and the radiation you should be cancer free."

Michael bit back the words *but for how long?*

They made the arrangements for the surgery, scheduled the pre-admission testing, and finally made their way to the car. His mother looked tired and shaken, but not beaten. A muscle jumped in his father's jaw. His parents held hands.

As he drove them home, Michael carefully asked, "Mom, the wedding won't be too much for you, will it?"

"No, honey. I don't have to do anything but attend the rehearsal, the dinner, and the wedding. Juliana's family is taking care of everything. Your father and I just have to go where we're told."

"You still have to smile and be surrounded by hundreds of strangers."

His mom peered at him intently. "Michael, you're not...upset... that Charlie's getting married before you, are you?"

"No. I'm just worried you'll be worn out by all the hoopla."

"I'm gaining another daughter-in-law. That makes me very happy. I'll be just as happy on your wedding day."

"Mom."

"Don't worry about the wedding. And don't breathe a word about the surgery to Charlie and Juliana. I won't have their day spoiled. This should be the happiest day of their lives."

At ten o'clock that night Michael turned off his computer and leaned back against his chair. He'd researched mortality rates for breast cancer recurrence, read anecdotal stories from survivors, re-read the theories about the power of positive thinking, and searched for more new treatments. His head felt stuffed with information. He felt drained, but he knew he had no chance of sleeping because his brain was wide awake.

He'd gone for a run with Jamal after returning from his parents' house where he'd stayed for dinner. Hell, he'd helped cook dinner and cleaned up afterwards. He was wired enough to need another run but not at this hour. Sex would work off his tension. Too bad he wasn't involved with anyone. He thought about Ileana—she'd wear him out but good.

But thinking about her only made him tenser. He pushed out of the chair and wandered his condo, his movements restless. He stared out the sliding glass doors at the water in the channel the complex abutted. A dock jutted into the water. He could go sit on the end of it and dangle his feet in the water. It was something he'd done with his brothers during family vacations when they were younger. The four of them would roughhouse on the dock until the inevitable happened and one of them tumbled into the water—usually Charlie. The rest soon followed, cooling off in the warm water because that's what boys did. Afterwards, they'd bear a scolding from their mom for spoiling the baths they'd had in the tub earlier. But they'd had so much fun together they hadn't cared.

They hadn't been four peas in a pod. They'd had four distinct personalities. But they'd been so close. His brothers had accepted his silent moods without question. No, they'd ignored the moods, acted like they didn't exist. They'd included him even while he brooded. He hadn't had that total acceptance in years. Not since Billy died.

Michael opened the door and stepped out onto the deck. The night sweltered, still trying to throw off the day's heat. He gripped the edge of the wooden deck. The scent of unchlorinated water, recently mowed lawn, and charcoal teased his nose.

Part of him had died with Billy, the part that could join in a rowdy group even while he was pensive. His brothers had closed up and closed him out. All the happy laughter and good times, the long distance calls that stirred warmth in his heart, had dried up in one fatal instant. Then he'd been completely alone. His friend Jamal couldn't take his brothers' place. No one could recreate the history he shared with his brothers.

He'd missed them a lot in the past two years. But he'd learned to live without them. That was his punishment for his failure as a big brother. But though he deserved his solitary state, he'd discovered recently that he resented his brothers moving past Billy's death. He resented them finding happiness and being able to build lives with the women they loved. He resented being on the outside now, no longer a part of their magic circle.

And he resented like hell that he had to carry the fear for his mother alone. He knew it was irrational and unreasonable. His brothers weren't ignoring their parents. They were just living their lives unknowing, while Michael got to carry this weight every day.

He had to stay positive to keep his parents positive because the mind could perform miracles. But he was no saint; he was just a man, a man with a sick mother. And even though he'd been independent for years, he still felt like a little boy inside and needed his mother's comfort. But she couldn't comfort him about this.

He returned inside to do sit-ups and push-ups until his gut ached and his biceps and shoulders burned. Then he took another shower and lay down on the cool bed sheets. Alone.

•••

The woman lay on a concrete surface as though asleep. But she was unnaturally still. She was young and pretty, her long straight hair, dark brown. She wore only mint green lingerie, her ample breasts nearly popping out of the lace cups. Her limbs lay loosely akimbo, as though she'd fallen. Her chest no longer moved up and down with her breaths, and because of that, someone else was in danger.

Ileana woke gasping. Automatically she turned on the light, reached for the little tablet and pen on her bedside table and wrote down what she could remember. It was the Sight. No dream felt like the Sight did when she experienced it, so incredibly real and vivid.

Ileana didn't know the young white woman and was unlikely to meet her because she spent her days surrounded by Cubans. She was sure the woman was dead, but how had she died? There was no blood, no wound. The woman looked peaceful, like she'd gone to sleep.

Ileana grabbed her robe from the end of the bed and wrapped it around herself. She always felt cold after the Sight. She'd only dreamed of death once—when one of her aunts died in a car accident. Why would she dream of this stranger's death?

She never dreamed of things unrelated to her or her family or their business. How was this woman linked to them? Could she be a customer?

Ileana didn't know all her neighbors. Could one of them be ill? Could one of them have been slipped a date-rape drug and died? Or OD'd on some other narcotic? But if that was the case, it didn't explain why Ileana had dreamed about her. A neighbor wouldn't usually trigger her Sight.

The last dream she'd had, had been of Michael, and he'd been a stranger. Was she going to meet this woman soon, maybe the live version so she could warn her? Ileana had to content herself with that.

Wide awake now, Ileana knew she wouldn't sleep. Michael's name had brought his image to her mind. Her body suffused with an all-over flush and liquid heat pooled in her lower belly. Although the Sight had prophesied Michael would be her lover, they had moved no closer to intimacy. Her Sight was faultless, so she wondered what would have to happen to change their relationship. Was the barrier her own self, her resistance to his race?

At times, she thought Michael yearned just as strongly as she did for a joining. At other times, he held himself coolly aloof, like he had after the phone call today. Maybe his mother's illness was the deterrent. His face had been strained during the call, his shoulders slumped as though weighed down by a burden. And what a burden. If her mother had faced cancer even once, Ileana would have been a basket case. She worried over her father's health; after all, high blood pressure could lead to heart attack and stroke. His mortality pressed on the edge of her awareness.

But cancer was a frightening disease. The word made people cringe. She'd thought Michael uncaring about his family, but today she'd seen he cared a great deal, he felt deeply, he loved his mother a lot. She understood that kind of love. She knew it intimately. And knowing Michael felt the way he did made her heart warm to him.

He must feel so alone. Something in her cried out for his pain and his solitary suffering. He'd rebuffed her offer of help. But perhaps the Sight had held a different meaning. Perhaps she was to offer him the comfort of her arms and her body. She knew about heartache and loss. She knew what it was like to writhe in her solitary bed feeling alone and disconnected from the world.

Michael could not turn to his parents for comfort. He needed someone. In his hour of need, she would offer herself to him. She could let him sate himself in her for as long as he needed her. Her body clenched in response. They'd have to meet secretly. Her family must not know. They'd never accept such wanton behavior...and with a white man.

Bold words in the darkest hour of the night. She hadn't dated in a dozen years. She knew what modern women did in the dating world, but she'd never done anything like that. How was she supposed to become Michael's lover?

Ileana huffed a self-deprecating laugh. Men knew what to do with a willing woman. She just had to let Michael know she was willing. He'd take it from there.

And take her. Over and over again. She knew from her dream.

In the morning, she would call him and accept his initial invitation for a date...a real one. Her mind made up, Ileana snuggled down into her covers. Roberto's picture smiled at her from the nightstand. He'd been an outwardly passionate man, in the first blush of real manhood when he died. He'd lit an equally passionate fire in her. Joy had sung through her veins for three short years before it had been snuffed out, along with all of her plans and dreams. They'd been soulmates, the halves that completed one another.

Since he died, she'd been encased in ice, living on the surface, but dead inside. Michael seemed Roberto's opposite—ice on the outside. Yet the Sight had shown her the passion inside him. And today, she'd glimpsed the depths of his soul. He could draw her from her icy prison, and she would do the same for him. Roberto would approve.

Although her body pulsed with need, she felt she could sleep now. The sooner she went to sleep, the sooner tomorrow would come.

CHAPTER 8

Michael made a ton of money that morning. Ruthlessly, he made deals and moved merchandise. Desiree raised an eyebrow at some of the order forms, but he shrugged off her curiosity.

He had to have liquid funds in case his mom needed something. If Dr. Ramos decided she needed a test, a procedure, if he changed his mind about them traveling to India, or if there was something not covered by his mother's insurance, he only had to tell Michael and he'd make it happen. Ramos knew it, yet he never abused Michael's largesse. Dr. Ramos ordered only those treatments and tests that would make Mrs. Ziffkin better. And for that Michael respected the man.

When Ileana phoned before lunch, Michael eagerly took the call, focused almost entirely on doing more business with the Calderons. Although a small part of him thrilled at hearing her voice.

"Hello Ileana."

"Michael, I need to talk to you."

"What can I do for you?" She sounded so serious. He hoped her father wasn't displeased with the new merchandise.

"Michael." She paused and then rushed on. "Michael, would you have dinner with me?"

Michael's thoughts derailed. "Dinner?"

"Yes, tonight."

"Sure. Where would you like to meet?"

"Um, could you pick me up?"

His thoughts raced like a hamster in a wheel. No, she couldn't be asking him out. She'd made it clear she wouldn't date him.

"At my house," she added.

His mouth dried. Visions of them twined together in bed flooded his brain, heating his blood and causing an immediate rise in his nether regions.

Stop it, he told his libido. *She's not offering you sex.* He licked dry lips. "I don't want to misunderstand. This isn't a date, right?"

"As a matter of fact, I've reconsidered and I'd like to go out with you."

Oh God, it was a dream come true. Yet it wasn't a dream he could make reality. Yesterday had shown him the reasons he couldn't get involved with Ileana. She wasn't a one-night stand, and he wouldn't lead her on about anything else.

"Ileana, I…"

"Do you like Italian?" she interrupted.

"Um, yes."

"Tony's on Seventh Street has wonderful stuffed ravioli. How does that sound to you?"

Any words spoken by her husky voice sounded like an invitation to sex, which this was not. "Um, that sounds delicious."

"Good." She sounded breathless. "Could you pick me up at seven?" She rattled off her address and he got caught up in writing it down.

"Seven, then? Can you find your way there?"

"Yeah."

"I can't wait. See you later." And she hung up before he could voice his reservations.

Ileana had asked him out! She'd been so adamant about them not dating that this about-face threw him. And all he could think about was sex.

He couldn't call back and cancel. Her family's business was more important than ever. He had to maintain a good relationship with the Calderon heir. At least that's what his brain said. But he'd accepted a dinner invitation and given a false impression. She thought they were going on a date while he needed to keep things casual between them.

•••

Michael had accepted! Nerves fluttered in Ileana's stomach. She felt flushed by her boldness.

Her office door opened and her father walked in. Ileana's cheeks burned with embarrassment. She was glad he hadn't heard what she'd just done.

Her father closed the door behind him and leaned against it. His face was stern. "Ileana, I have just spoken to Manuel Hernandez. He says you told Emilio you are still in mourning."

She should have expected this sooner. "Because I am, Papá."

"Ileana, you must stop this. You are still a young woman and it is time for you to do what all young women do, to become a wife and begin a family. Emilio is a good match."

"I know that, Papá. But he doesn't call to my heart. You said you understood."

Her father's face mottled with red. "I want this for Calderon, child of my flesh. This thing the doctor insists on—this exile from Calderon—is not my choosing. I fear it makes Calderon vulnerable. I do not wish the company my father started to be put in such a position. A connection with Hernandez would strengthen the company. Can you understand this, Ileana?"

She gripped her hands together. "Yes, Papá."

"A Calderon president looks out for the company's best interests."

"If you choose me to succeed you, I would do that."

"But while I am still president I ask this of you...for Calderon. For the family."

"You ask too much," she said in a small voice.

"Yet you were prepared to do it once before."

He meant with Roberto. "That was another time." And she was another person.

Her father looked at her for a long time, saying nothing. He was not used to being defied openly like this. Perhaps he thought his mere presence could quail her into submission.

He thought wrong.

Finally he sighed. "Will you come to the house for dinner tonight?"

Ileana tried not to flush. "I'm sorry, but I have plans tonight."

His dark eyes narrowed. "Another business dinner?"

"No."

"Very well. Any progress on the break-ins?"

"Not yet. I believe they're tied to the one at Citadel though. I spoke to Michael Ziffkin about it."

"When?" he fired at her.

"Yesterday. He told me to talk to the police."

"But they were no help."

"I know. But I told them our suspicions anyway. That's all I have so far."

"Keep working on it."

"I will."

When her father left, Ileana's shoulders slumped with relief. If he knew what she planned with Michael tonight, she'd never know peace.

She was pacing her house, unable to sit for long, when Michael's Mazda sedan pulled into her driveway. Her throat dried. Her pulse went haywire. As he stepped from the car, she dropped her purse. He was so dark and sexy and masculine in his double-breasted black suit. Her body cried out for him, for what she knew he could do to her.

As Michael strode up the walk with a long-legged stride, she bent and snatched the purse from the floor. Darting to the door, she opened it to find his finger poised to ring the doorbell.

"Sorry I made you get out of the car. I dropped my purse." Oh, that sounded bright.

"A gentleman escorts a lady to the car."

A Cuban man would. She liked his manners. She liked the way his mouth quirked in a small smile even more. His lips looked kissable.

Michael stood close enough for her to feel his body heat, yet not as close as she needed. Within his arms was where she really wanted to be.

She didn't imagine the heat in his dark eyes. He wanted her, too. She knew what desire looked like and Michael was wearing it. They didn't need to go out to dinner if they'd already gotten to this point. Why not go straight to bed? How did modern women invite a man into their bed? Twenty-nine years of Cuban breeding held her tongue silent.

"Did you forget something?" he asked.

How to breathe. How to think. How to seduce a man. "No," she replied instead.

"Then we should probably go."

No, they shouldn't. But she allowed him to urge her out the front door to his car. He opened the car door for her, again standing close. She slid into the coolness of the still air-conditioned car, tucking her full skirt inside. She looked up to find him watching her movements with palpable intensity. Her body sang. Why didn't he suggest they go back inside?

But he closed the door instead. She sighed. It was going to be a long evening until they arrived back here where Michael could make a move.

Ileana couldn't help watching Michael as he drove, so she saw him swallow, take a deep breath, and wipe his palm along his black trousers. He was nervous. No wonder he hadn't acted on the heat in his eyes.

He glanced at her. He did feel what she felt. It excited her.

At the restaurant, he opened her door for her. His palm against her lower back was welcomingly warm. Her nerve endings tingled with pleasure. His nearness created flutters in her stomach. His glances over her body were bold—like a caress that stroked her nipples—and yet restrained. His restraint frustrated and yet endeared her to him. It reminded her of the Cuban males that populated her life, yet he was different enough to thrill her.

Ileana couldn't say what they ate or what they talked about. His deep, calm voice stroked her nerve endings. She'd never known a voice could enthrall her, but Michael's did. She could listen to him talk all day...and all night. She thought if he'd had an accent—British or Australian—he probably could make her come just by speaking.

She flushed.

His dark gaze was knowing. A smile teased the corners of his mouth, which caused her stomach to clench.

Ileana watched his hands; his long fingers were sure. They stroked the water glass. Her gaze darted to his eyes. He knew she watched him. She couldn't tell where his pupils ended and his irises began—all was molten heat.

Oh my. She swallowed hard.

Michael reached across the table and stroked one long finger down the back of her hand. Electricity jolted through her and she jerked in her seat. Her breath came in small pants. His gaze dropped to her quickly lifting breasts. Her breasts tingled. When his gaze rose to meet hers, sexual awareness zinged between them.

"Are you ready?" he asked, his tone husky.

"Yes." Any more ready and she'd come with his next touch.

He rose. She did too, although her legs felt shaky. She'd welcome lying down...with him.

Ileana was close enough that she heard the buzz of his vibrating phone and saw Michael twitch. Without looking away from her, he withdrew it from his trouser pocket. His breath hitched. He glanced at the display quickly and then frowned.

"Pardon me. It's my security." He pressed her up against him with his free palm.

Her nerves jangled all along where her skin met his.

"Ziffkin." Michael listened. He stiffened against her. "Who is it?"

Ileana felt his attention shift completely, and then he took a step away from her. "How'd they get in?" he barked.

Something niggled at her subconscious, something more than this scene being a repeat of their last dinner together.

"I'll be right there." He jabbed the off button.

"Another break-in?" she asked.

Michael ran a distracted hand through his short hair. "No, but I need to go. I'm sorry. Again. I'll pay for your cab home."

"I'll come with you."

"No," he snapped, then gentled his tone. "Security found a dead woman in my warehouse."

Shock rocketed through Ileana. Her eyes widened and she knew she must look frightened because Michael wrapped his arms around her.

"It's all right."

She nodded, unable yet to speak. She had a suspicion her dream from last night was about to come true. And she had to know: was the dead body a beautiful woman in her underwear? If so, the danger she sensed in the dream was to Michael and his business.

"I'm coming with you."

CHAPTER 9

"I'm coming with you." Determination showed on Ileana's face. Her cat-slanted eyes dared Michael to gainsay her. Hell, he wouldn't do that. He wanted her with him too badly.

As they walked to his car, he sighed with frustration. He'd been certain the evening would end differently because she'd been giving him the green light all through dinner. He couldn't believe the change in her since their last meal together. He was sure she wanted him as much as he wanted her.

But now the mood was ruined. A dead body. How had this happened?

Michael was hyper aware of Ileana as he drove as fast as he safely could through Miami's nightlife traffic. His semi-arousal pulsed in his too-tight slacks, reminding him of what wouldn't happen tonight. He shouldn't be taking Ileana with him. He risked so much in doing so. He had to remember she represented an important client and he needed her company's business.

And if tonight scarred her psyche, he risked never knowing the hot sweet succor of her body.

He gripped the steering wheel with violent force. These incidents had to stop. If he got his hand on the perpetrators, he'd take out his frustrations and anger on them.

The police were already on the scene when Michael arrived at his warehouse. The red and blue lights strobed the Miami night, painting the structures on both sides of the street.

One look at Ileana's set face told him no argument would sway her, but he had to try. "You should stay in the car."

"I'm coming with you." Her stubborn streak was deeply rooted.

He stopped arguing, but kept her close.

The security guard, John Tessla, met him at the door. John's face looked like he'd made a habit of losing boxing matches. "The police told me I could let you in, but only you."

His flat gray eyes slid to Ileana, where they widened slightly in appreciation. "I'm sorry, Mr. Ziffkin. I didn't know you were busy."

"It's okay, John. This is Ileana Alvarez Calderon. Ileana, one of my security team, John Tessla."

The two nodded at one another and exchanged greetings.

"Miss Alvarez Calderon can wait with me," John suggested.

But a glance at Ileana showed the mulish set of her face. "She'll go with me. It's okay. I'll handle the police."

Michael followed the sound of muffled male voices inside to the cops' location. He'd braced himself for anything except what he found—a pretty brunette in dusty green lingerie lay sprawled on the concrete. There were no marks on her that he could see.

Ileana gasped. Her face paled. He pulled her into the warmth of his body.

The cops turned. "You're the owner, Michael Ziffkin?" the taller one asked.

"Yes."

"We're officers Turner and Martinez," the shorter Latino cop, who must be Martinez, said. "The lady may want to wait outside."

Since Michael knew that wasn't an option, he ignored it, instead asking, "What happened?"

"Drug overdose," Turner, the white cop, answered. "Cocaine. There's white powder in her nose. Do you recognize her?"

Michael shook his head. "I've never seen her before."

"Were any of your employees working tonight? Maybe she was partying with them. Drugs and sex sometimes go together. She looks like a high-priced call girl, so maybe it was one of your married employees."

"Other than my security team, none of my employees was scheduled to work." Michael tried not to stare at the young woman. She had large breasts that amply filled the lacy bra. Her dark thatch was evident through the lacy panties. He wished Ileana wasn't standing here. He wished he wasn't, either.

"It seems an odd place for a sexual tryst," Michael remarked, forcibly not looking at Ileana. Now it seemed sordid that he'd had sexual thoughts about her the day he'd met her. "If this girl was a professional, you'd think she'd take her John to a hotel room."

"Sometimes illicit thrill enhances the experience," Turner said. "And if your employees are dealing drugs out of your warehouse, and she was trading sex, what better place to do it?"

"My employees aren't dealing drugs here," Michael retorted with force. No, not that.

"We'll have to investigate that angle, Mr. Ziffkin," Martinez said. "After all, she died on your premises."

God, he didn't need that kind of negative scrutiny.

"And if it was an accidental OD, why did whoever was with her run?" Turner added.

Worse and worse. Michael looked around and cleared his throat. "Where are her clothes?"

"We haven't found them," Martinez replied. "Whoever was here might have carried them off to hide her identity."

"She looks like a co-ed," Michael blurted. "Not a drug addict."

"I don't think she was a co-ed." Ileana's quiet voice broke the sudden silence.

Michael stared at her. She shuddered. Quickly he slipped out of his suit jacket and wrapped it around her shoulders. She closed her eyes, inhaling, and snuggled into his jacket. He tried to ignore how her actions aroused him. When her brown eyes opened, she gave him a look of approval, which caused warmth to spread through his chest.

"Why do you think that, miss?" The last word of Officer Martinez's query contained an additional question as to her identity.

"I'm Ileana Alvarez Calderon. I have the Sight, inherited from my maternal grandmother. I dreamed of this woman last night. I sensed danger."

At the cops' disbelieving frowns, she continued, "You don't have to take my word for it. I recorded my vision in a notebook. You're welcome to look at it or interview my family about what I've told you. My visions have never been wrong."

"Was there anything else in your dream?" Martinez asked. "My great aunt had the Sight."

"No. I woke up disturbed because I almost never dream about strangers."

"It wouldn't hurt to call Homicide," Martinez told his partner.

While the cops made the call, Michael drew Ileana outside. He was still reeling from her revelation—the Sight. His brother Rick's wife saw the dead. Charlie's fiancé could find objects by touching something related to them. How bizarre that Michael should also meet a woman who had psychic abilities. He'd never believed in psychics, but his brothers accepted that aspect of the women in their lives.

As he turned to Ileana, he found her staring at him, her brown eyes clear, her gaze unwavering. He realized she was waiting for his reaction to what she'd said. She looked the same as before—sexy, exotic, desirable. Her pronouncement was simply another layer of the things he was learning about her. She lived in a world apart from his. Of course some of her beliefs would differ from his. He was glad she was different.

A compulsion he could not deny made him lower his head to hers. Her brown eyes widened. Her lips parted with a puff of warm breath just before his lips touched them. Hers were warm and soft. They molded to his as though made for him. A groan slipped from him. He had to fight the urge to grip her hard and rip the form-fitting dress from her body, so he could bare her tender flesh to his desires. He wanted to take her right here and now, fusing their bodies so they could never be parted.

With a soul-jarring wrench, he lifted his head. He was panting as though he'd run a mile. Ileana's face was flushed, her eyes filled with desire. Their circumstances came back to him in a rush. This was not the time or place.

"I'm sorry. I shouldn't have done that," he said.

"I'm not. I enjoyed it."

He took a step away from her so he wouldn't kiss her again. But he so wanted to.

The medical examiner and homicide detectives arrived within minutes of one another. Michael, Ileana, and John Tessla stood within view and earshot of the proceedings. The detectives mentioned getting the narcotics squad involved. Michael couldn't believe that a young woman who looked like that would choose to come to a warehouse in this section of town in order to do drugs and have sex. It just wasn't logical.

Ileana leaned against him and he wrapped his arm around her. He couldn't help noticing she fit perfectly in his arms. He nuzzled her silky hair, breathing in the scent of something exotic and spicy.

Michael heard footsteps coming towards them and John heading away to meet whoever it was. Michael let security deal with it. John would chase off gawkers or the press. A moment later, two sets of footsteps approached them. Must be more police.

Michael turned and looked straight into his brother Rick's eyes.

CHAPTER 10

Michael's gut tightened like it had every time he'd seen his brother since Rick moved back to town six months ago. Michael tensed, wondering why his brother was here. As far as Michael knew, this wasn't Rick's territory.

"Rick. What are you doing here?"

His brother looked relieved. "I heard about a possible homicide at Citadel. I was worried." For a moment the echo of Billy's ghost haunted Rick's brown eyes. Then he took in the woman in Michael's arms. A dark eyebrow lifted in query.

"As you can see, I'm all right." Michael's arm tightened around Ileana. "Ileana Alvarez Calderon, this is my brother Rick Ziffkin. He's a homicide detective with Miami PD."

Ileana held out her hand and Rick shook it. "It's nice to meet you. Michael mentioned your wife is having a baby. Congratulations."

Rick beamed. "Thanks. We're pretty excited about it."

"I'm sorry about..." Ileana began.

Michael suddenly realized what secret Ileana knew that Rick didn't. He gripped her forearm. "Ileana, no."

Her startled gaze flew to his. He shook his head slightly.

Rick frowned, looking back and forth between them. "Sorry about what?"

Ileana searched Michael's face. He knew she didn't understand. How could she?

"It's nothing," Ileana answered.

Michael relaxed his grip and rubbed her arm in apology.

"I should find out what the detectives know," Rick offered. He moved to the group around the body where handshakes then ensued.

Michel took the opportunity to pull Ileana out of earshot. "My parents don't want my brothers to know. Rick's got the impending baby to worry about, and Charlie's getting married next weekend. My mother doesn't want them to worry."

"But they have a right to know."

"It's my mother's decision, not yours." The words came out more sharply than he intended. When Ileana raised her chin, he tried to smooth things over. "I'm sorry." It didn't help that he agreed with her.

"I'd be so hurt if my father kept his health problems a secret from me."

"It's only for a little while. She wants them to be happy."

Ileana reached for his hand. "What about you?"

It was a rapier thrust to the heart of the matter. "I'm their oldest son. They depend on me."

Her smooth palm cupped his cheek. He was nearly felled by the tenderness of that touch. "You're a good man, Michael Ziffkin."

He couldn't help it then. He gathered her against him until her heart beat against his. She wrapped her arms around him. He leaned his cheek against her hair and sighed, closing his eyes. He would gladly have stood like that forever, but minutes later someone cleared his throat.

Michael sighed, lifted his head, released Ileana, and faced his brother. "What did you find out?"

"It's possible the body might have been dumped here. There's a small needle mark in her arm, but not junkie tracks."

"You mean somebody dumped her here because she OD'd?"

Rick inhaled. "No. We think somebody might have killed her and left her here."

"To implicate Citadel in drugs?" Michael demanded.

Rick frowned. "Do you suspect something?"

"I had a break-in at one of my warehouses the other day. And merchandise turned up missing at another warehouse. Now this. I don't think it's a series of random events."

Ileana gripped his arm. "If you do business with Mohamed Abdul as well as with Calderon and Hernandez, your buyers are being targeted, too." She explained the other break-ins to Rick.

"It sounds like I'm being softened up for protection money. Maybe the whole industry is. It'd be a great way for the mob to move drugs, too."

"If that's true, Michael, you could be in danger," Rick said.

"Nonsense," Michael scoffed. "It's Citadel's money and connections they want."

"You are Citadel. There's no board, no corporation. There's only you. That makes you vulnerable."

Michael tried to hide his surprise that Rick knew anything about his business. He'd thought his brother was wrapped up in his new wife and gestating child. "This is all conjecture anyway. It's just a gut feeling. I have no proof."

"I'll notify the major crimes unit. They'll want to talk to you. Probably as soon as the M.E. rules on cause of death." Rick looked over towards where the black body bag was being lifted onto a gurney. "Maybe sooner."

"I'll tell them what the families know," Ileana offered.

"Families?" Rick asked.

"Cuban-American merchant families. Calderon is the oldest and strongest."

"So you met through business?" Rick mused.

"Yes," she said.

Michael had to stop his brother from probing deeper. After only one date, he and Ileana couldn't explain what they were to each other. "Should I take Ileana home or do you think major crimes might want to talk to us tonight?"

Rick didn't look fooled by the change in topic. "I have a friend over there. Let me call him." He pulled out his cell phone and stepped away to make the call.

"You don't have to do this," Michael told Ileana.

"The police need to know what we know. You want to protect me because I'm a woman, but right now I represent Calderon."

Michael smiled at her. He liked her gutsiness. It reminded him of his mom. Wouldn't that surprise his mother? The thought sobered him. He wasn't planning any kind of long-term relationship with Ileana. He didn't know what Ileana had in mind, either.

"This has been a crazy evening," he mused.

"Just like last time," she agreed.

"How did you foresee our evening ending?"

The small smile that tugged at her lips, combined with the sultry look of her cat-slanted eyes, made lust kick Michael in his lower body. He began to harden.

He swallowed. "I don't want to misunderstand."

"I don't think you do," she purred.

He prayed the cops wanted to talk to Ileana and him in the morning.

But God hadn't been answering Michael's prayers lately. Rick returned to announce, "My friend will meet you at the Front Street station. I'll follow you down there."

"You don't have to," Michael objected. "I know Analise isn't feeling well."

"She's not going to sleep until I get back. There's a full moon tonight. She wants to visit some friends later and dance in the moonlight."

Michael frowned at his brother's smile.

"We're going to the cemetery," Rick explained. "The ghosts like to dance by the full moon."

"I don't understand," Ileana said, frowning.

"His wife talks to the dead," Michael explained.

Ileana stared at Rick. Her mouth opened in an O-shape. Before she could make inquiries, Michael guided her towards the door. He told John Tessla where they were going and to lock up after the detectives were finished.

In the car, Ileana spoke. "Your brother seems nice."

"Yeah."

"Does his wife really talk to the dead?"

"She says she does and Rick believes her. He's never seen any ghosts but he says he's felt them."

"How do you feel about me having the Sight?"

How did he feel? Slowly he explained. "I have no first-hand experience of the supernatural. I never believed in it before. Yet now I have a sister-in-law who talks to the dead. I'll soon have another who can locate stolen objects with her mind. You say you dream what will happen. I guess anything's possible."

"Thank you for accepting it."

Michael shrugged. "About Rick. He's going to be curious about you and me. We've only had one date, and, well...I like my privacy," he finished.

"I think I understand. Are you close to him?"

Michael sighed. "Not anymore."

"Did something happen?"

"Yeah."

"Can you talk about it?"

Michael watched the traffic while he waited for the red light to turn green. He knew Ileana was staring at his profile. "We had a younger brother, Billy. He was a brilliant biochemist working in a research lab. He said he was going to cure cancer some day." *Don't think about that.* "But he was murdered two-and-a-half years ago in New Orleans in a robbery gone wrong. They never found his killer."

"How awful. Rick is a homicide detective. He couldn't solve the case?"

"He wasn't one then. I think he became one to help. But even he couldn't find out who did it."

"And you blame him?" she gasped.

Michael glanced at her. "Hell no." No, he blamed himself. "But Billy's murder broke us up. It was hard to talk to one another afterwards."

"That's sad. Families should be a source of strength in troubled times."

"Ours wasn't."

"And this is what's between you and your brother? You seemed so tense with him."

"That's part of it." Michael's jaw hurt from gritting his teeth. He didn't want to spoil their time together by pouring out his bitterness. Ileana didn't need to hear it. "Can we talk about something else?"

"Sure."

• • •

Ileana could only guess at the source of the conflict between the brothers. They were equally intense, but Rick smiled more freely. Of course, he didn't know about his mother's cancer. Michael bore that heavy burden alone.

She knew families could be dysfunctional. She saw it on TV and heard about it, but she couldn't understand pushing away the people you loved during a time of grief. She'd wanted to die with Roberto, but her family had wrapped their loving arms around her. They'd sustained her through those terrible hours, days, and weeks after the car accident. She would not have made it without them. How had the Ziffkins survived?

At the precinct, Rick led them through the warren of offices to a medium-sized room crammed with desks. The walls were covered with tack boards, themselves sheathed with photos and other papers. Rick introduced them to Detective Paul Washington. Ileana couldn't guess his age from his clothes—black jeans and a multi-colored pullover. He was as bald as a cue ball.

They pulled chairs up to the detective's cubicle and told their stories. He took notes. He did a computer search for the related case files and printed what he could. With the pieces laid out together, it did seem to have an organized feel to it.

When Detective Washington began to ask Michael detailed questions about his business, Ileana wandered over to the water cooler.

Rick joined her there. "Have you known my brother long?"

"Not long," she demurred.

"That's probably why he hasn't said anything about you."

"Probably. Michael is intensely private."

Rick glanced towards his brother. "He's intense all right."

Here was a perfect opportunity to learn more about Michael. "Has he always been so?"

Rick looked back at her. "Yeah. I think it's the oldest child syndrome. You know, it's just them and the adults until the other kids come along. There's so much burden on the oldest, expectations and such, and that parental learning curve."

Ileana smiled at him. "Reading up on fatherhood?"

Rick actually blushed. "Sorry. Analise and I have never been around kids. We want to get it right."

Ileana was sure he would. "You're the second son?"

"Right behind Michael, but I'm two years younger. I think Michael was a lot for my mom to get used to. Billy was after me." His happy glow dimmed for a moment then reasserted itself. "Last is Charlie. Michael was our protective older brother."

"And you all live in Miami?"

"Now we do. Charlie and I came back home this year. Michael was the only one who never left."

Ileana wanted to know about the friction between the brothers, but she had to tread carefully. "Do you see Michael often?"

Rick looked over at his brother and frowned. "Not really. He's gotten very quiet. He used to brood when he was younger, but we'd rope him into playing with us anyway. Now," Rick shrugged. "I can't get through to him."

He glanced at his watch. "I have to go. I don't want to interrupt. Would you tell Michael I'll see him at the rehearsal dinner, if not sooner?"

"Rehearsal dinner?"

"For Charlie's wedding. It's next Friday night. Are you coming?"

"Michael hasn't talked about it."

"Tell him I said to bring you. I'll see you around." He strode out the door, taking his ready smile with him.

Ileana refilled her cup of water, got another one for Michael, and slid into the chair beside him. She placed his cup on the desk in front of him. He gave her a grateful smile and returned his attention to his discussion with Detective Washington.

Ileana listened distractedly to them while she mulled over what Rick had said. And what he hadn't said. He wanted to regain what he'd lost with Michael, but his brother wouldn't let him in. Michael was the protector, but Rick was the one who'd gone into law enforcement.

Michael had stayed here and protected the home front. He'd allowed his brothers the freedom to follow their dreams. And while they were chasing dreams, one brother had died. The family had fallen apart. His mother had gotten cancer. How did Michael feel about all that had happened? Ileana was sure that was the key to understanding him.

Two more detectives drifted into the room and joined the discussion. They outlined scenarios and suspects until Ileana began to yawn. A glance at her watch showed her it was one-thirty. No wonder she was tired. And she had to be up at six.

Michael noticed her next yawn. "I need to take Ileana home. Have we covered everything, Paul?"

Detective Washington nodded. "We'll work on the problem some more, and I'll call you with our plan of action."

"Good."

Michael rose and pulled Ileana up. Outside the station house, the late night chill raised goose bumps on her arms. The ride home seemed surreal—traffic was extremely light and the streetlights streamed in her sight as the car sped towards her home.

This wasn't how she'd envisioned her evening ending. She'd been awake nearly twenty-four hours and felt brain dead. She no longer felt sexy or alluring. What would Michael expect when they arrived at their destination?

Her nerves jangled. Seduction plans seemed so much easier to carry out when she was fresh and hadn't been faced with a dead body and hours in a police station.

When the car pulled into her driveway, her mouth dried. She licked her lips. Her pulse throbbed in her body. What if Michael wanted more and she was too tired to perform? What if he'd lost interest?

He opened her car door and walked her to her front door. She felt awkward and nervous. She didn't know what the right thing to do was.

"We're both tired," Michael said.

Ileana nodded. Her tongue felt thick, her brain even thicker.

"I'd like to try again sometime. See if we can make it through an evening without a call to the police."

Her smile felt forced. "That would be nice."

There was a fraught, awkward moment during which she wondered what Michael was thinking.

"I should go," he said.

Disappointment seared through her.

"Ileana..."

"Michael..."

They spoke at the same time.

"Hell," he swore.

He reached for her biceps and pulled her into his kiss. The flame that had been simmering flared up into an inferno. His kiss transported her to another time and place where lips alone were all a person needed to sustain them. She found herself gripping his back, but didn't recall putting her arms around him.

Michael ripped himself from her arms. Cool air bathed the front of her body where a moment before there'd been intense heat.

"We can't do this now. You're exhausted. We both have to work tomorrow. We haven't even had time to talk about what happened tonight. All we've had time to do is react. We're still reacting."

Ileana made a sound of protest.

"We are. We've had some emotional shocks. It's normal to want human comfort, to want to lose yourself in a warm body, but I won't do that to you. I don't want you to regret being with me..."

"I wouldn't."

"I want you to be able to say no if you want to. Right now I don't think you can."

Ileana didn't think she could either.

"So I'm making the best choice for both of us." He backed up one step and then another. Then he turned and hurried to his car.

Michael waited for her to go inside before he drove away. Despite her fatigue, she wasn't sure he'd made the right choice for them.

CHAPTER 11

The next morning Ileana dashed through the front door of Calderon nearly two hours late for work and almost ran her father down.

"Papá!"

"Ileana. You missed the staff meeting this morning."

"I know. Carona called me. I'm sorry. I fell back to sleep after my alarm went off." She continued walking towards her office. Her father kept pace with her.

He came into her office with her and closed the door. Ileana's muscles tightened, but she continued putting her purse in her desk drawer.

"Ileana, is there anything you need to tell me?"

She looked up. "Like what, Papá?"

"You've never overslept before. Perhaps my job is too much for a young woman."

"That's not it at all," she denied with vigor. "I was at the police station until one-thirty with Michael Ziffkin..."

"Ziffkin? Why?" he demanded, his face reddening.

"If you'd let me finish. We may have determined the reason behind our break-ins. It may be organized crime..."

"The mafia? How can that be?"

Ileana told her father about the dead body and the major crimes unit. The only things she omitted were dinner and the heat between her and Michael.

Her father sputtered, "But you should not have gone anywhere near where someone might have been murdered. What were you thinking?" His voice rose at the end.

"I was trying to do the task you assigned me. I thought there was a connection to the events at both our companies. You told me to solve it."

"I did not tell you to risk yourself or to involve yourself with Ziffkin."

"I wasn't at risk."

"Why were you with him?" he demanded, his tone authoritative.

She'd never lied to her father, so she couldn't think of a lie now. "We had dinner together. I didn't tell you because I knew you'd be angry."

"Are you spending as much time with our other suppliers as you are with Ziffkin?"

"No, but he's our largest supplier."

"Calderon has always maintained a strictly business relationship with its suppliers. These dinners between two unmarried people send the wrong message. You should have said no when he asked."

"I asked him."

"What?" her father nearly roared.

"Papá, you're so old-fashioned. Women do that now."

"I won't have you inviting men to dinner and certainly not Ziffkin. I forbid it." His face purpled dangerously, and he was visibly perspiring.

"Papá, your blood pressure!" Ileana hurried around the desk to him.

He fought off her attempts to make him sit down. "Forget about my blood pressure. No daughter of mine..."

"I'm calling your doctor." Ileana reached for the phone, alarmed by his state.

"I do not need the doctor."

"You need to calm down. The doctor said no stress."

"You caused my stress. You and your wanton behavior."

If he only knew. But she'd been circumspect in public. "I'm hardly wanton, Papá." When he continued to resist, she decided to pull out the big guns. "I'm calling Mamá."

"Not your mother!"

"Yes. If you won't be calm, she'll know how to handle you."

He poked his thumb into his chest. "I am the head of this family!"

"Not for long if you keep up this tirade."

Her father huffed several breaths, glaring at her. "You defy me."

"I don't want you to die, Papá. Not over this."

His expression softened a little. "I am not going to die. Your worry is excessive."

"So is yours."

Her father narrowed his eyes. "You will obey me in this."

Ileana said nothing.

Her father seemed to make up his mind about something and nodded. "I will leave you to your work."

Ileana watched him leave and wondered who had won that round. She didn't understand why she felt the need to stand up to him over Michael, but she did. She'd only defied her father a few times in her life—when she went to college and lived in the dorm, when she moved into her own home on the very edge of the Cuban neighborhood, when she refused to marry without love, and now over Michael. What did Michael have in common with the major decisions of her life?

• • •

"Esteban Calderon is here to see you," Michael's secretary announced over the intercom.

Ileana's father was here? Michael frowned. He thought the man was turning over the reins to his heir-apparents.

"Send him in." There was only one way to find out what the head of the Calderon Consortium wanted. Michael stood and straightened his gray suit.

Nadine opened the door to admit a stocky, black-haired man around sixty years old. Michael had met Esteban a number of times since he'd founded Citadel.

"Thanks, Nadine." She smiled and closed the door. Michael held out his hand. "It's good to see you again, Mr. Calderon."

Esteban didn't offer his hand in return. "I do not want you to see my daughter again."

Michael stiffened. "Pardon me?"

"You heard me. She told me she was with you last night. I have told her to stay away from you, and now I am telling you."

"Nothing happened with Ileana..."

"And nothing will. She is of a fine Cuban line. When she marries, it will be to a Cuban."

Michael felt compelled to protect Ileana. "What does Ileana have to say about that?"

"Ileana will do what is best for Calderon. She knows her duty."

Calderon's attitude was extremely outdated. "This is the twenty-first century. Women marry who they choose."

Esteban poked his chest with a thick thumb. "Cuban women marry who their father says they may marry."

"Ileana has a mind of her own."

"That is why I have come to you. You will obey me in this because you like my business."

Michael's belly went cold.

"You like all the Cuban families' business. I see you understand. I thought you would. Ileana is not used to being at the top of a company, of interacting with men of power outside the Cuban community. She has a curious mind. She likes to learn new things. She may display interest in you, but she does not mean anything by it. She is an innocent, you understand?"

Michael didn't think her father knew Ileana at all, and she certainly wasn't innocent. She'd be angry if she knew her father was here now having this conversation.

But Esteban knew Michael wouldn't tell her. If Michael had learned anything about Ileana, it was how important family was to her.

Could Michael afford to lose the Cuban business? What a question and what a time to face it. He knew the answer was a resounding no. But could he give Ileana up? He'd sworn he wouldn't start anything with her, but after last night...

Nothing had happened. And now nothing was going to happen. There was no choice really, not while his mom had cancer.

"You don't have to worry, Mr. Calderon. I want the Cuban business."

Esteban's eyes had gone cold. "I am glad you are a reasonable man, Mr. Ziffkin." He held out his hand. "I have your word on this?"

Michael felt like he was moving through setting concrete when he reached for Calderon's hand. "Yes, you have my word."

After Calderon left, Michael asked Nadine to hold his calls. Then he sank his head into his hands. He'd never had a chance with Ileana anyway. He didn't want any kind of commitment. But his head filled with images of her—her cat-slanted eyes, her face dazed with passion, her quickness to help the detectives in major crimes, her incisive mind grappling with the mystery of the break-ins, her concern over his mother overflowing onto him when he needed it. She was a rare diamond—exquisitely beautiful and priceless, breakable, in need of protection, sharp enough to cut through the hardest surfaces, flawless, covetable.

And he had to throw her away.

Work would have to be his salvation. Perhaps it wouldn't hurt to seek new customers just in case Calderon decided to keep Michael on a short leash or punish him. There was a reason he'd never mixed business with pleasure before. Perhaps a road trip down the coast was in order—a prospecting trip for new clients. He liked that idea. It put him out of Ileana's and Rick's reach and far from pre-wedding festivities. Even better.

Michael searched out all the tourist shops in Florida that weren't his clients and began classifying them into types of prospects. Then he began making calls to set appointments with decision makers.

A few hours later, he answered the phone to find his mother on the line. "Hi, Mom."

"Michael," she sounded a little breathless. "Do you have something you want to tell me?"

"Mom, you called me."

"Honey, why were you keeping Ileana a secret?"

Damn that blabbermouth Rick. "Mom, we had one date."

"Your brother said you two could hardly keep your hands off one another. I've been so worried about you, especially after your brothers both found someone to love."

Oh God. Michael would give her anything she needed, anything but this. "Mom, I don't think I'll be seeing her again."

"Oh, Michael, what happened? Were the crimes too much for her? And Rick thought she was a strong woman."

Ileana was. A spine of steel, a heart of gold. "I'm sorry you got your hopes up. Rick shouldn't have said anything to you."

"He was happy for you, Michael. So was I. Are you sure you can't work something out? I was hoping to meet her at Charlie's wedding."

"Mom, I wouldn't ask a woman I'd recently begun dating to a family wedding anyway."

"Think she might get ideas, Michael?"

Well, yeah. "It's a moot point now. But I'm glad you called. I have to go on a sales trip..."

"Oh, Michael, now?"

"It can't wait. Unless you need me here."

"Your brothers might need you. Charlie might get nervous and need to talk to his big brother."

"I've never been married. I couldn't give him any advice. Besides, he wants to marry Juliana."

His mom sighed. "You're running away. Did this Ileana hurt you? Is that why you're making yourself scarce?"

His mom was closer to the truth than she knew. "My business needs this sales trip. The wedding festivities don't require my presence. You'll need me next week, so I have to go this week."

"Fine, but you'll be back for the rehearsal dinner, right?"

Michael made a quick decision. "I'm not in the wedding, so probably not. But I'll be back by Saturday."

"Michael!"

"You'll call me on my cell phone if you need anything, right?"

"Of course."

"This week won't be too much of a strain on you if I'm away, will it?"

"I'd like your presence. So would your brothers."

"That's not what I mean."

"I know. Go on your sales trip. You always had a mind of your own."

"I'll see you Saturday, Mom."

Now that he had a goal, Michael notified his staff and security and Detective Washington. Then he finished setting appointments and went home to pack. Prior to the evening rush hour, he was on the road north. He was sleeping alone tonight and every mile he put between him and Miami made sure of it.

That night he called Jamal from his lonely hotel room.

"Hey, Michael, Desiree said you left on a trip."

"Yeah. I had to get out of town."

Jamal laughed. "You can't escape the wedding hoopla forever."

"It's not that. Well not all of it. Jamal, I had to make a bargain with the devil today."

"What kind of bargain?"

"You have to swear not to tell Desiree."

"I don't like to keep secrets from her."

Michael stood and pulled the window curtain aside to look out at the parking lot. "This is important. I'm her boss. She can't know this. Are you where she can't hear you?"

"Is your company in trouble?"

"No. Maybe. You know I have a lot of Cuban clients."

"Yeah."

"One has a daughter. I've seen her a couple of times. We had a date."

Jamal snorted. "You? A date?"

"Yeah." Michael took a few deep breaths. "Her father found out. He threatened to pull his business if I didn't stop seeing her."

"My God, can he do that? It sounds so archaic."

"Yeah, him and all his Cuban friends who are also clients."

"Could your company survive that?"

"I don't know. Times would be really lean for awhile. I'd pretty much have to start over again."

"So is this woman worth it?"

Michael sighed. "I promised him I wouldn't see her again. I shook hands on it."

"Jesus. Your first date in years and you traded her for your business."

That stung, but it was the truth. "Jamal, my mom's cancer is back."

"Oh, God, I'm sorry to hear that. How's she doing?"

"She has to have another mastectomy next Monday. But if she needs anything that I have the power to give her, my business can't be in trouble. Her health might depend on it. I had to promise him."

"Oh, Michael, that was rough. I'm sorry, man."

Michael missed the water behind his condo. He closed the curtain. "Would you have done what I did?"

"I'm not you. My mom's not sick."

"If she was, would you have made the promise?"

"Given up Desiree?" Jamal inhaled. "No. But I'm in a committed relationship. You said you only had one date. Love and commitment make a difference. I wouldn't give up Desiree for anything."

So, since Michael wasn't committed, he'd done the right thing. So why did it feel like the wrong thing?

CHAPTER 12

Michael was avoiding her. Three days without a phone call made Ileana sure he'd been scared off. She knew he ran hot and cold, which she now attributed to a dichotomy between his mind and his emotions. When he felt too much, he withdrew to analyze and reorient. And they'd nearly blown the lust-o-meter the other night. He'd begun pulling back from her at her door. She should have seen the retreat coming. But she hadn't and it hurt.

She felt completely alive for the first time since Roberto died and she wanted to revel in it...with Michael, the man who made her feel all sorts of things.

But he wouldn't give her the chance.

She'd waited patiently for him to call. Then she'd given him time to brood. Now she was tired of waiting. She wanted to be with him again.

Ileana called his office. "I'd like to speak to Michael Ziffkin please."

"Mr. Ziffkin's out of town. If it's important, you can leave a voice mail. He's checking them. Or maybe his assistant, Desiree Carver, can help you?"

"He didn't tell me he was going out of town." Ileana had been so wrong. But why hadn't he called from wherever he'd gone?

"A sales trip came up suddenly. He'll be back in the office on Tuesday, next week."

"This is Ileana Alvarez Calderon. May I have Michael's cell phone number?"

"I'm sorry, Miss Calderon, but we don't give out Mr. Ziffkin's cell. Would you like to leave a voice mail?"

Ileana sighed with frustration. "Yes." She asked him to call her, then hung up and stared at the phone. How strange.

There was a knock on her door and her father entered. "I need those sales projections I gave you yesterday."

Ileana dug on her desk, pulled them out and handed them to her father. He'd looked much healthier the past few days.

"Oh, Caridad has invited the family to dinner. My grandson, Rafael, won a trophy at his swim meet today and your sister wants everyone to help celebrate. Are you available tonight?"

Ileana scanned her calendar. "Yes, I am."

"Good. Seven o'clock then." Her father looked terribly smug.

When he left, Ileana wondered about that look.

Hours later the phone rang. "Ileana Calderon?" a woman asked.

Ileana held the phone in the crook of her neck. "This is she. How can I help you?"

"My name is Jane Ziffkin. I'm Michael's mother. He asked me to invite you to his brother's wedding."

Michael's mother! Ileana nearly dropped the phone. "Why didn't he ask me himself?"

"You might be nervous about accepting, it being a family occasion and this being your introduction to the family. I wanted to extend the invitation myself, let you know how welcome you'd be."

"Thank you, Mrs. Ziffkin. That does make me feel less nervous. I understand all about family occasions. I come from a large, extended family."

"I've wanted to meet you ever since I heard about you."

"I've wanted to meet you, too. I've been praying for you ever since Michael told me about your cancer."

"Michael told you?"

Ileana smiled. "Yes. He loves you very much. I think you're a brave woman."

There was a poignant pause on the other end, then, "I can't wait to meet you."

• • •

Late Friday night Michael called his parents. "How are you, Mom?" He braced his cell to his ear.

"Tired. The rehearsal dinner was delicious. You should have been there. The Sanchezes are the most delightful family. Juliana's half-brothers are precocious. They remind me of students I've had."

Michael stretched out on the hotel bed trying to loosen too-tight muscles. "Mom, everybody reminds you of some student you taught."

She chuckled. "When you've taught school as long as I have it's inevitable. When will you be home?"

"Probably late tomorrow afternoon. I want to get in as much business as possible."

"Michael, you're going to be exhausted for the wedding."

"I don't have to show up until the rest of the guests."

"You could show up earlier to be with your family." Her voice was tart.

"I'd be in the way."

"You sound tired."

"I am. I've had to be at my sharpest for days. Had to prove myself and my company to skeptics. Had to coerce and cajole and then make it all happen."

"You're driving yourself too hard."

"It's my company, Mom. It's going to rise or fall on my actions."

"Who will you leave it to, Michael? Why are you working so hard if in the end you have no heir?"

Michael's chest tightened painfully. He'd never felt as alone as he had these past few days. A thousand times a day he'd fought the urge to call Ileana, to hear her voice. He'd promised.

"There's plenty of time for an heir, Mom."

"It requires a special woman."

"There's time for that, too. Mom, I have some work to do before I go to sleep. I'll see you tomorrow."

"Sure, honey."

But when Michael hung up, all he could think about was the special woman barred from him.

•••

Michael paced the narthex of St. Mary's Church. He'd escaped his brothers' almost painful attempts to draw him into their pre-wedding chatter. The harder they tried, the more trapped Michael had felt until he'd fled. He'd stopped himself from leaving the church altogether. His mother would never forgive him for that.

He watched the guests arrive and the ushers seat them, but he couldn't sit still yet. Nothing was as it should be. He couldn't feel comfortable with the brothers he'd known and loved for years. He couldn't join in their banter. Rick and Charlie acted like they'd never been separated. But Michael felt differently. His brothers weren't strangers...and yet they were. He'd lost what he used to share with them.

Damn it, he'd thought he'd accepted he would never have a day like this. Why, then, did he want it to be him in the sacristy joking with his best friends as he counted down the minutes until he was bound forever to the woman he loved?

His parents appeared from the dim corridor where Michael knew the bride and her attendants did last minute fussing. His mom and dad had aged well. They were a handsome couple. Michael's heart swelled with love and pride.

His mother smiled at him. She was putting on a brave front today. No one would know what she faced less than forty-eight hours from now. She loved Charlie enough to keep him ignorant so he could have this day.

Michael wished he could have that ignorance today too. He turned away...

And found himself facing Ileana.

She was so beautiful. The sleeveless red dress made her look utterly feminine and very desirable. The full skirt showed off her long, tanned legs. She took Michael's breath away, robbed every thought from his brain save one—he wanted her. Not just physically, although his body had come painfully alive when he saw her. He wanted her tucked protectively within the circle of his arm. He wanted to feel her palm smooth his cheek, wanted to lean his forehead against hers and stare into the depths of her warm brown eyes.

It had felt so long since he'd been with her, and yet had it been only four days?

"Ileana." Her name slipped like a benediction from his lips.

She smiled warmly and crossed to him. He couldn't move. Then she reached up on tiptoe and kissed him, and nothing else existed. The world melted away. How had he survived four days without her kiss? Why had he thought he should?

As she ended the kiss, it all came flooding back—Esteban Calderon's horrible pact and Michael's oath.

Michael stiffened. *Oh my God.* "Ileana, what are you doing here?"

CHAPTER 13

"What are you doing here?"

Whatever emotion had raged like a flash fire between Ileana and Michael shattered into a million pieces with his tortured question, which sounded more like an accusation.

Hurt doused her lust like ice water, quieting the fire she'd felt only with him. Embarrassed heat flamed her cheeks as she noticed the older couple taking in the scene. They were probably his relatives.

How could she have misjudged the look of welcome on his face, in his lips? Surely she hadn't been alone in the searing passion of that kiss.

Another glance around showed the older couple still standing at rapt attention. Farther down the hall, a flock of pretty bridesmaids emerged from a room. Behind Ileana, the outer door opened and several people stepped inside. Oh God, this scene was going to play out in front of witnesses.

Oh, why had she come? Why had she thought Michael had... Wait a minute. "You invited me."

"No, I didn't," he denied with some heat.

"I did," the older woman admitted, stepping forward. It was the voice from the phone call. "I'm Jane Ziffkin, Michael's mother." She held out her hand to Ileana.

"Mom," Michael protested. "How could you?"

Ileana, caught between mother and son, took the proffered hand. "Mrs. Ziffkin, I don't understand."

The man who must be her husband looked as confused as Ileana felt. Up close, she could see he shared Michael's eye and hair coloring. Michael, however, had his mother's thinner bone structure.

"I wanted you here," Mrs. Ziffkin explained. "With Michael."

"Mom, you don't understand."

"I understand what I observed when you saw this young woman. Your reaction was more honest than you've been with me."

What had he said to his mother?

"Whatever the problem is, it's resolvable if you're together."

Problem?

Mrs. Ziffkin still held onto Ileana's hand. The bridal party was fast approaching. The ushers hovered by them with earnest, urgent faces. They were holding up the proceedings.

Then Mrs. Ziffkin captured Michael's hand and tugged him close enough to slip his hand into Ileana's. An electric current jolted through their joined hands. Ileana looked up at Michael, but he was turned to his mother.

Mrs. Ziffkin kissed him on the cheek. "This makes me happy." She stepped away to take an usher's arm.

In that instant, there was such pain on Michael's face that Ileana ached for him.

His father leaned close. "Do as your mother wants, son. Give her this day." He patted Michael's shoulder and followed his wife and the usher down the aisle.

The bride—a lovely Latina in a princess style dress—and her rainbow of attendants, including two little Latina girls, all stared at Michael and Ileana.

"Michael, you need to be seated," the bride stated, her voice serene.

A tall Latino man in full police dress uniform moved up next to the bride. "Is there a problem, Michael?" His glare said there'd better not be.

Michael's hand gripped Ileana's harder. "No sir, Captain Sanchez. My date has just arrived."

"Then you'd best find your seats. Your brother's waiting."

"Shall we?" Michael offered Ileana his free arm.

Ileana swallowed her questions and laced her arm through his. Michael ignored the usher and walked her down the aisle. She was aware of faces turning as they passed, of his mother's brilliant smile, and of the two dark-haired men in tuxedos entering the front of the church. Other young men entered after they did, but it was the first two who drew her attention. One was Rick, who stared at her and Michael with intense interest. The other man—clearly the groom—was a more beautiful and vibrant version of Michael. Would Michael look like that if he smiled readily?

Then Michael reached the family's pew and they scooted in past his parents. His mother squeezed Ileana's hand as she passed.

The wedding march played, the congregation stood, and Ileana watched with tears in her eyes as the bride approached. She always cried at weddings. Michael's arm stole around her waist, and she rested against his warm, hard frame until the bride reached the front of the church.

As the traditional wedding Mass unfolded, Ileana wondered why Michael had chosen not to be a groomsman. Instinctively, she knew it had been his refusal; it wasn't that he hadn't been asked. Why did he separate himself from his brothers? Rick had chosen to stand with Charlie, acting as his best man. Any barriers between those two had been breached. But Michael was still imprisoned inside his walls.

As though he couldn't help it, Michael kept his arm around her or held her hand all through the long Mass. Ileana caught his mother eyeing their joined hands. Then she wiped away tears and leaned against his father. Ileana didn't think Michael had caught the byplay.

When they bowed their heads to pray, Michael nosed the hair at her temple, sending goosebumps up her arms. She didn't believe he was acting for his mother's sake because his mother wasn't even looking. She was wrapped up in her youngest son's exchange of vows.

All these years Ileana had listened to wedding vows, feeling the poignancy of her own unrealized dream. Roberto had not lived long enough to marry her. They would never have a home filled with dark-eyed Cuban children, never grow old loving each other. Now another dark-eyed man sat beside her barred in his castle of pain and sorrow, a man capable of deep love, a very human man who could be hurt.

The bride was Hispanic, the groom white. There were many Latinos on the bride's side, yet there were whites, too. Cops of all races in dress uniform were sprinkled liberally on both sides, another unifying factor.

Ileana eyed the man beside her. When had she forgotten he was white and had simply begun to think of him as a man? He was complex with many interesting facets. And he was far from perfect, but she didn't want perfection.

Michael caught her perusal. His eyes were pools of liquid chocolate, his expression severe. He leaned closer and captured her lips for a too-brief kiss. But it was enough to make it hard to breathe.

Then the Mass was over and they waited in the pews to be released.

"It was a beautiful ceremony," Mrs. Ziffkin said, swiping a tissue under her eyes.

"They make a stunning couple," Ileana agreed.

"Her family lived next door to ours until she was sixteen. Her father broke them up when he caught them in bed together. He even moved away to keep them apart. But Charlie and Juliana were made for each other."

What a difference Charlie was from Michael, then.

"Michael and Charlie were as different as night and day," Mrs. Ziffkin said, as though she'd read Ileana's thoughts. "I wondered if

Michael had a sense of humor, and I doubted Charlie had a serious bone in his body. Well, except for his acting. He took that very seriously. But now Charlie has found some balance. Michael... well, there's still hope." She gave Ileana a meaningful look.

"I can hear you, Mom," Michael said over Ileana's head.

"I meant you to," his mother retorted then turned as Charlie and Juliana arrived to free them from the pew.

"Oh, Charlie, I'm so happy." As his mother hugged him, Charlie's smile outshone the sun.

Everyone in their pew exchanged hugs, kisses, and congratulations with the newly married couple. Juliana was as radiant as Charlie. Ileana could see they loved one another. She watched closely as Michael congratulated his brother. On Michael's part, the hug was stiff. When he hugged Juliana, however, he was more natural. Then their little group made its way to the back, leaving the bride and groom to greet people in the next pew.

Michael drew Ileana and his parents into the side hall with Rick. His mother hugged and kissed Rick. When Michael and his father stood side by side, the resemblance was startling.

"Do you want to sit down?" Michael quietly asked his mother.

"I'm all right. Don't worry." She patted his cheek then took hold of one of Michael's arms and one of Ileana's. "Want to tell me what happened between you?"

Ileana frowned. "When?"

"Mom." Michael's admonition was stern.

But his mother ignored him. "Why you broke up when it's clear you're crazy about each other."

CHAPTER 14

"You broke up with me?" Ileana exclaimed. "When?"

Michael rubbed his face with his free hand and cursed his mother—silently of course. Cancer didn't give her liberty to meddle where she didn't belong, even if she was right about how he and Ileana responded to each other. This was no way to tell Ileana.

"This isn't the time or place," Michael insisted. "We have a few hours of reception still to get through." He looked at Ileana. "Unless you want to leave?"

"Absolutely not," his mother snapped, her gray eyes blazing. "I forbid you to spoil Charlie's day."

"You're right. I should go." Ileana's cheeks reddened like her dress. Hurt and anger warred in her eyes.

"No!" his mother intervened. "I invited you. I want you to stay. Please. For me."

From the look on Ileana's face, she knew his mom was using her cancer to get her way. And Ileana was going to cave. What had gotten into his mom? She'd never done anything like this before. All she would succeed in doing would be to hurt Ileana and frustrate him.

"All right. I'll stay," Ileana agreed.

Michael wanted to growl his frustration. He wanted to kiss those beautiful lips, lift that full skirt and thrust his body into hers until she knew how he really felt about her, and he also wanted to be on the other side of the room so he wouldn't be tempted with the forbidden fruit. He couldn't tell her either what her father had done or how Michael had chosen between his mother and Ileana. Guilt and self-loathing ate at him. And despair.

Michael caught his mother staring intently at him and quickly smoothed his face. She had teacher radar where secrets were concerned. He and his brothers had never gotten away with anything, and more than half the time, they confessed under her scrutiny. But she would not break him this time.

Rick wedged himself into their midst. He had his arm protectively around his wife, a hugely pregnant young woman with black hair and pale skin. "It's nice to see you again, Miss Calderon. I wanted to introduce you to my wife, Analise."

Ileana and Analise shook hands. Except for her belly, Analise was a petite woman dwarfed by Rick's height and breadth. Yet they looked like they fit well together. And they glowed with love for each other. A sharp pain stabbed Michael in the stomach. No, he was not jealous of Rick's happiness.

"Rick told me about you," Analise said to Ileana. "I'm so glad you came."

Ileana glanced at Michael and guilt ate at him again.

"Are you feeling all right, dear?" his mother asked Analise.

"I'm fine. I wouldn't miss this for the world."

"The doctor's talking possible bed rest," Rick blurted, despite Analise's shushing motions.

"Bed rest," his mother exclaimed, alarm clear on her face.

Analise gave Rick a disapproving look. "It's precautionary."

"Then by all means sit down." Michael's father set a chair behind her and gently pushed her into it.

Mrs. Ziffkin frowned. "Maybe Rick should take you home."

"Nonsense," Analise exclaimed, putting her hands on her belly. "I'm only having a baby. It's not like I'm sick or anything. Jane, tell your son how when you had cancer you didn't let anything stop you."

Michael sucked in his breath. He heard a similar sound from Ileana. His mother's face fell for only a moment, and then she rallied.

"You're right, Analise. I lived life to the fullest. But that's my first grandchild you're carrying. Precious cargo, you know. Handle with care."

Rick and Analise looked at one another with such love that it hurt Michael to see it. It hurt him more to know his mom was putting her own worries aside to take care of them.

"I'll lie down while they're taking pictures," Analise promised. She hugged Mrs. Ziffkin.

During the photo session, his mom assigned Michael and Ileana to watch Analise and make sure she rested. Although he was grateful for the third party, which prevented the discussion he knew Ileana wanted, the looks she shot him spoke volumes; he wished his sister-in-law were anywhere but here. The sooner he set Ileana straight, well, the sooner they could get over this obsession they seemed to feel for each other.

But Analise fell asleep almost immediately, her head pillowed on Michael's suit jacket. He and Ileana would have to whisper in order not to wake her.

They watched the photo setups like two strangers. Charlie and Juliana glowed like tiny supernovas with their newfound happiness. They'd met again this winter and within two weeks had gotten engaged. Rick glowed too. He and Analise had met, fallen in love, and married less than two weeks later. Both his brothers had found instant happiness. Well, technically, Charlie had grown up with Juliana, but he hadn't shown romantic interest in her until they reached puberty. And then her father had put an entire town between them.

Michael had felt instantly attracted to Ileana. The ache in his pants was a constant reminder of her nearness. Staring at her feminine profile made him even harder—those full, immensely kissable lips, those surprisingly round, proud breasts, the small waist, the full skirt under which she wore no panty hose—he'd checked. What he wouldn't give to be alone with her in one of those darkened rooms down the hall. He'd sit in a chair and lift her over his lap and let her slide slowly down onto his cock. He'd fill her sweet body while clutching that small waist in his hands.

On the upward movement, he'd stop her so he could suckle those outthrust breasts.

God, his hard-on was painful.

Ileana turned to him then, and whatever hunger was on his face made her mouth drop open. Slowly she licked her lips. Her eyes glinted with her desire. He got even harder. He wanted to kiss those lips, spend hours tasting and nibbling them, and let her taste his own.

He extended his arm across the top of the pew. Ileana extended hers to meet his. Her touch electrified him. He stroked the top of her silky hand with one finger. Her brown eyes were very bright. Then he stuck his finger in his mouth to wet it and slid it between her thumb and index finger. Her eyes widened. He slid the finger in and out, telling her what he wanted to do to her. In and out—if only they were alone. In and out—if only they were naked. In and out—if only he was on top of her pressing her into the bed.

Her chest heaved with her breaths. He wanted to see her breasts move while she lay naked under him, jiggling heavily with his powerful thrusts. Her nipples pebbled under the thin red fabric. Her gaze fell to his tented slacks and stroked him with a look.

"To hell with the reception," he whispered.

"We promised your mother. Besides, we have to talk."

"We are talking."

"Talking dirty."

"You seem to like it."

"So do you." Ileana indicated his hard-on.

"If we're not going to leave, we shouldn't talk like this."

"Oh, I think I'm going to keep on with this discussion."

"Don't start what you can't finish."

"Put your money where your mouth...is." Her sultry look could have seduced a saint.

Michael pictured all the places on Ileana's body he could use his mouth and the ways she could use hers. His hand spasmed around hers.

"I'll see your bet, and raise."

Again he pictured her in his lap riding his dick as his hands on her small waist lowered then raised her...then lowered her once more.

"I call." His voice was hoarse with arousal.

"I bet you do." Her voice was throaty.

"I want to see what you have."

"Tonight, if you're lucky."

If only he could. Maybe they could be together once to scratch this itch. If it was only once, no one would have to know. It was a powerfully tempting thought.

"What are you two talking about so intently?" his father asked from the pew in front of them. When had he sat down?

"Poker," Michael answered straight-faced.

Ileana choked and began coughing.

"They're talking dirty," Analise said, stretching and sitting up.

His mother's eyes twinkled wickedly. Michael's face burned.

"Someone else was talking dirty to you?" Rick demanded of his wife in patently pretended outrage.

"Not *to* me. *Over* me. It got me all hot and bothered, and in my condition."

Rick pulled her out into the aisle and into his pew and his lap. "That's my job, honey." He kissed her hard and then glared at Michael. "Have you no shame, man? You're in a church." He laughed and Analise giggled.

"I think your brother would like a few minutes alone with Ileana," his mom suggested, bless her.

Rick snorted. "A few minutes alone now and she might end up in the same condition as Analise."

"Richard," his mother chided.

Michael's face burned even hotter. He hoped his mom couldn't see what condition he was in. How mortifying that would be. A glance at Ileana showed her face was equally red.

His mother studied their faces. "Maybe we should go straight to the hall."

"Good idea," his father agreed. "The newlyweds are ready to leave. We'd best see them on their way."

...

The reception reminded Ileana of her own family's weddings. Although the Sanchezes were of Mexican descent instead of Cuban, the Latin influence was similar. Ileana felt at home with the large and boisterous Sanchez clan and the sprinkling of Spanish words they spoke to each other. If only there wasn't this unrelieved tension between her and Michael. If she hadn't promised Mrs. Ziffkin, Ileana would have invited Michael home with her prior to the reception.

Whatever reason he'd had for allegedly breaking up with her, it wasn't that he found her undesirable. Definitely not. Those looks he'd given her in the church could have melted her panties. Michael wanted to have sex with her in a bad way. And damn if she didn't want it, too—very badly.

Ileana was afraid if too much time passed that Michael would cool down or think his way out of going home with her. Despite popular thinking that weddings were contagious, this reception was dampening Michael's mood.

He was polite and overtly friendly to his family. He'd been overly solicitous to his mother until she said something to him that Ileana couldn't hear. Then he'd clammed up and his tension had begun to increase.

After that, the family dynamics told her what she needed to know. Both brothers had new wives and looked ecstatic with happiness. They smiled a lot. Their mother couldn't be happier for them and with her daughters-in-law. But in the midst of the revelry, Michael sat unsmiling. Despite her presence, he was alone. He shared in his brothers' joy only peripherally. When it was only him and his parents, the mood grew more serious.

Ileana caught an expression of anger on Michael's face so fleeting she wasn't sure she'd labeled it correctly. He was watching Rick laugh with Charlie. Then she realized what was going on. Michael's brothers got the happiness while Michael got the worry. And she was pretty sure it wasn't the first time. He was angry because he had to carry the anxiety alone. That was the wedge between him and his brothers.

Ileana admired and liked Jane Ziffkin, but she thought the woman was wrong for withholding knowledge about her health from her other sons. She'd placed an unfair burden on her oldest. He probably felt like he carried the world's problems on his shoulders. No wonder he was so serious.

The band had begun a slow song, and Ileana decided on a course of action to lighten Michael's mood. "Would you dance with me, please?"

Michael frowned. "I don't really dance."

"You know how, don't you?"

"Yes," he admitted with reluctance.

Ileana held out her hand. She noted they were alone. "They say dancing is like making love while standing up."

His dark eyebrow lifted. He placed his hand in hers. "Then by all means let's find out if it's true."

Michael held her pressed tightly to him and, oh, it felt good. All her cells, muscles, tendons, and bones sung with joy. His lithe body telegraphed every move he made as they navigated the dance floor. Her body took directions like it had found its master. His erection was a welcome invitation pressed into her abdomen, rubbing between them as they moved. He kept a long leg between her thighs as he turned her, pressing her intimate folds against him until she gritted her teeth in frustration at the need for more intense contact there.

Michael nuzzled the side of her face, nipped her earlobe, blew in her ear, and pressed her breasts into his chest until she was light-headed. He stroked her back with his fingertips, down to the curve of her butt, to the edges of her breasts and down her sides. She tried not to moan or melt into a puddle on the dance floor.

A salsa dance came next, but they did not release one another. Their movements were lurid, sensual, wanton, excited. And when their steps parted, she flaunted her body for him, wiggling her hips and jiggling her breasts. Michael thrust his hips in imitation of the act they both wanted. She'd never danced a salsa with such heat before.

"Soon," he whispered against her ear.

"Sooner," she pleaded, biting his ear. She had to make love with him or she'd go mad.

Yet he made her dance the next song—a flamenco. On the dip, he ground his erection between her thighs and she gasped as her lower body clenched. There were a few abandoned twists and turns, and then he did it again. Ileana groaned with need.

The flesh on his cheeks was flushed and tight with arousal. The bulge in his pants was huge and hot.

When the dance ended, Michael grabbed her hand and dragged her back to his family.

"That performance was X-rated," Rick commented.

"We're leaving," Michael announced. His voice sounded like grinding metal.

"I don't doubt it," Rick muttered.

His mother said nothing when Michael kissed her cheek, but her eyes were knowing. Ileana blushed and kissed his mom, too. His dad gave Michael a long, telling look.

They said good-bye to the newlyweds and fled the hall. "I'll follow you home," Michael said.

"Did I invite you?" she inquired, just to be naughty.

"Hell yes you did."

"Took you long enough to get the message."

"That was foreplay. Now I mean business."

CHAPTER 15

The click of the front door lock sounded like a starter's pistol. Ileana could barely catch her breath from the excitement of knowing she and Michael were about to make love.

Michael pressed her against the front door with his hard, eager body and kissed her hungrily. As always, Ileana went up in flames. She wrapped her arms around him as he fumbled between them. He yanked her skirt up and her panties down then got his trousers undone. She helped by sucking on his tongue, pushing him to rough, desperate movements. She liked his urgency, knowing how much he wanted her. His hot penis slid between her legs, along her already moistened folds and she welcomed it there where she ached. He slid the head back and forth and pressed it against her opening. It had been so long since she'd been intimate with a man and it felt wonderful. She rode his length as he prepared her for entry.

"Condom," Michael requested, breaking away from her lips and panting hard. His penis thrust faster through her folds.

"What?" Ileana tried to recapture his lips.

"I don't have a condom. Where do you keep them?"

Cold reason caught up to her brain. "I don't have any."

Michael stopped moving. His body vibrated with tension and his chest heaved with his breaths. "I won't risk getting you pregnant."

"Michael, it's okay..."

"No it's not. I wouldn't do that to you."

She covered his lips with her finger. "I know how to give pleasure without intercourse. I know how to use my mouth and hands."

He groaned. "So do I."

"Good. I want this." She licked her lips and admitted, "I wanted you all evening."

"I wanted you since I first saw you." Michael nipped her ear.

She shivered. He ran his tongue down her neck and she arched her breasts into his chest. Her nipples were already hard and tight.

"And then you asked why I was there," she reminded him. Now that rationality had entered the room, she had time to think.

Michael pulled away to stare at her. "I meant the very first time. In my warehouse."

Her breath caught. "I wanted you then, too."

"What are we doing about all of this wanting?"

"Not enough." She caught his hands and raised his palms to her aching breasts. He squeezed them and sensation shot deep into her lower body.

"I've dreamed of what I want to do to your breasts." He planted kisses up the side of her neck.

"Do it. All of it." His thumbs rubbing her nipples felt so good she pressed up on her toes to get closer. She wanted her clothes off and his hands on her bare flesh.

Michael chuckled against her neck. "I will."

"Now!" she ordered.

"Impatient," he breathed, but he released her breasts. Ileana nearly groaned with frustration and need.

But Michael found the back zip of her dress and drew it down. Then he pulled the dress down to her waist, tugging it off her arms. Halting Ileana from yanking it the rest of the way, he said, "I have a fantasy that involves a chair and that dress half undone."

Her breath caught. It strangled in her throat as he unsnapped her bra and pulled it off. "Sounds interesting."

"Ah." He admired her breasts. "Beautiful." He palmed them, rotating his hands just enough to ease the ache.

"More," she begged.

"Touch me, too," he responded.

Ileana unbuttoned Michael's shirt and caressed his chest, until she found his erect nipples. Then she rubbed them, making him groan. He slid his cock back and forth between her legs again. She pressed her legs together, which increased the friction.

They both groaned.

"We have to be careful," he warned. "I want you so much. I want to be inside you."

"I want that too."

"I could go buy condoms."

She gripped his arms to prevent him from doing just that. "I don't want you to leave. Not tonight."

His answer was to capture her lips in a passionate kiss. Her hands slid from his arms to his tight, round buttocks. She pulled him tight between her legs again and again.

Michael groaned deep in his chest.

Ileana's lower body clenched with a needy ache. She made urgent noises against his lips. One of his hands left her breast. Finding her clitoris, he began to rub. All the places he was stimulating her coalesced into one hot throb of pleasure. She cried out as orgasm swept over her. Michael stroked her the whole time until she drooped against him.

Ileana felt the tension in him and caressed his buttocks. Then she moved her hands between them as he slid his penis from between her legs. It filled her hands, hot with his life and virility and slick from her body. She stroked his length and he groaned. She found his heavy sacs and fondled them with one hand while her thumb traced the head of his cock.

Michael's fingers plucked hard at her nipples, the little stings of pleasure and pain caused her womb to clench again. Her hands moved more quickly on his cock and testicles, stroking him towards his own orgasm. Michael threw back his head with a groan. He gripped her nipples hard. His hips thrust into her hands, urgent in his need. His orgasm spurted over her hands.

His groan sounded almost painful. When he finally relaxed, he dropped his forehead to hers.

"You do know how to use your hands." He smiled and her stomach flipped.

"I'm going to use my mouth next. Do you need a minute?"

Michael laughed and then groaned. "Let me use mine first."

"How would you like to use the bed?"

"Oh yeah."

He stripped off his pants and she led him into her bedroom. She locked the door, which earned her a raised eyebrow. "My family has keys to the front door. They don't have a key to this one."

Michael sobered. "Do they drop by unannounced often?"

"Often enough that I installed this lock. I'm Cuban, after all, and close to my family. But I don't expect anyone tonight."

He stood quietly, looking at the pants and underwear in his hand. "I shouldn't be here."

"Do you want to go?" It wasn't what she wanted.

Michael looked from his semi-erect cock to her fully erect nipples. "No. I want you."

"Then take me. You said something about using your mouth."

Afterwards, Michael lay on his side next to her in bed. He gathered her into his arms and kissed her. "That was wonderful. You were wonderful."

"It will be even better when we have condoms." But at her words she sensed his withdrawal.

"This can't happen again."

Ileana raised her head, stunned with disbelief. How could it be the end? Her dream hadn't even come true yet because he hadn't been inside her. "Why not?"

"It just can't. Tonight has to be enough."

CHAPTER 16

"What do you mean 'tonight has to be enough'? We just got started. This was the best night of my life." Ileana's voice rose. She wrenched out of Michael's arms and sat up in bed facing him.

The sated feeling left Michael, replaced by a tension that tightened his shoulders. He sat up, too. He'd been reacting since he saw her in the church, so he hadn't had time to think of a plausible reason they couldn't be together, but he couldn't lie to Ileana. She wouldn't believe him anyway after what they'd done to each other. Unless he acted like a real bastard.

But he couldn't do that either.

"I can't see you again and what just happened has to be our secret."

"Michael, what are you talking about? What's going on?" Ileana crossed her arms under her naked breasts. The sight was hugely distracting.

"I'm not capable of anything more than this." He waved around the rumpled bed. There, the truth, although not the truth that mattered.

But Ileana's face softened. She reached for him. He wanted to hold back, but his body went on autopilot into her arms. She lay back against the sheets bringing him with her.

"I know you're afraid," she said.

"I'm not afraid." Well, that wasn't exactly true.

"Michael," she chastised softly.

There was something decidedly wrong with this situation. His body was hardening again in response to the naked woman in his arms and he was telling her they couldn't ever be like this again? Hell, he couldn't foresee a time when he wouldn't want to get naked with her. He had it bad for her.

"I can't do a relationship," he admitted.

"You can if you start slowly. Baby steps."

"We've already had oral sex. We skipped the baby steps."

She smiled at him. "Did you want to go slower?"

"Hell no. Waiting to get you naked was killing me." He shouldn't think about that in this position. He had almost a full hard-on already.

"You're not making any sense."

"I can't make sense when your breasts are pressed against me."

Ileana rubbed the hardened tips up and down his chest. He gripped her hips and ground himself against her. How could he not be sated—he'd had two orgasms already. He'd taken her in every way save one. Maybe that was the reason—until he'd had intercourse with her he'd always want her.

"Why don't you have any condoms?" he growled to himself and her, thrusting between her legs.

"Why would I when I don't date?"

Michael froze. "What do you mean? You've done this before."

"Sure I have. With my *novio* when I was seventeen."

He knew she was close to thirty now. "I don't understand."

"My *novio*, Roberto Herrara, died when I was seventeen. A *novio* is like a fiancé. We were to be married. He was my *novio* from the time I was fifteen. I've been in mourning since then."

"And you don't date? At all?"

"That's what being in mourning means."

His mind couldn't process what she'd said. She'd given herself to him, was in the act of giving herself again to him, when she'd been in mourning for nearly a dozen years. She hadn't looked at another man with lust until him.

And he had to give her up?

Hell no. No, he had to have her. So he brought her to orgasm with his mouth and hands once more and let her do the same to him.

As they lay gasping afterwards, Ileana's muffled voice came from beneath him. "Why didn't you have a condom?"

All his defenses were down when he answered. "I haven't had a date since my brother died."

•••

Michael and Ileana showered and changed the sheets together. She didn't argue when he said he was staying the night. He'd been vulnerable and they both knew it. He needed loving arms around him and she was happy to provide them. He couldn't or wouldn't talk about how his brother's death had changed him. She knew some of the ways. It was enough for now that he stayed after he'd made his admission.

He kept touching her, as though he couldn't help it. They woke twice in the night when Michael tried to enter her, scrambling to separate in time, and then they pleasured each other with hands and mouths, a hint of desperation in their couplings.

When Ileana finally woke, it was late-morning and she felt thick with sleep.

Michael stood beside the bed with his clothes in his hands. "I have to go."

She reached for him. "Come back to bed."

He avoided her hand. "You're sore and I don't think I can get it up again today."

"Come back to bed anyway."

"I have to go to work…"

"It's Sunday."

"I've been gone all week and I'll be out of the office tomorrow."

"Why?"

Michael hesitated to tell her. Suddenly her mind fog lifted and she knew. "Your mom?"

He nodded. "She's having a radical mastectomy tomorrow. I'm sitting with my dad during the surgery then with her afterwards."

"I'd like to come with you."

Mixed emotions crossed his face. "Thanks, but no."

"I'd like to be there for you."

"I can't. I told you that. This has to be good-bye."

Ileana scrambled from the bed, dragging the sheet around her body. She would fight for what they had. "It's not good-bye. I won't let you throw away what we have because of fear."

"And I won't let you hang onto me. I can't. It won't work."

"Why not?"

"It's too big a risk."

"And you don't risk. Not since your brother died."

"No. I can't afford to."

He was throwing away what they had. That had been more than pleasure between them in her bed last night. That had been two souls bonding…just like it had been with Roberto.

"We're not finished, Michael. You want to know how I know? I dreamed about you, with the Sight. I dreamed we were lovers, but not like last night. In this dream, you were inside me. That hasn't happened yet."

Frowning, Michael insisted, "It was just a dream."

"But it's going to happen. My dreams always come true."

"My worst nightmare might come true if I see you again. I can't risk that."

"You mean that someone you love might die?"

Michael inhaled and paled.

Ileana reached for him but he stepped back. "I can't."

He turned and took a step towards the door. Despair stabbed her. He wasn't willing to risk losing someone he loved. Time slowed as he took another step. But Michael didn't love her, so he didn't risk losing her. Who would he lose if he continued to see Ileana? He loved his parents.

What would he lose? Fragments of memory stirred.

Her father's smug face.

Michael's fear in the church when he asked, "What are you doing here?"

His insistence that last night had to remain a secret.

Her father's smug face.

"What did my father threaten to do to you if you kept on seeing me?"

Michael froze, stiffening. "What are you talking about?"

"Did he threaten your business?"

He stood there as the clock ticked the moments away. Then his shoulders slumped. He turned back to face her. "Yes. Now you see why we have to say good-bye."

"No. Now I know how to fight for you."

CHAPTER 17

"You can't fight your father over me and win," Michael said in amazed frustration. "He's the head of Calderon. He makes the decisions. And his opinions sway the other Cuban families."

"My father doesn't always dictate what I do."

"You have nothing to lose. He's part of what's most important to you. He won't exile you from the family."

"I have something he values. It gives me a bargaining tool."

"What could you possibly have that would make him forget I'm not Cuban?"

"The keys to an empire. Through me, my father wants to unite Cuban businesses."

"But I'm not Cuban," he repeated.

"There are other ways to further his interests, like vertical integration for one."

Michael had trouble breathing. She had not just proposed to him although she'd certainly proposed a merger of some kind. She was ready to defy her father and basing that rebellion on certain assumptions, like a relationship between them lasting.

"What are you suggesting? That Calderon would sell to me, because I'm not in the market to sell Citadel."

"I thought more of two principals in the same industry choosing to make a commitment to a joint venture where both benefitted. An exchange of promises. Sharing of assets."

It sure sounded like marriage. "We hardly know one another. We don't know what the future holds."

Ileana looked at the bed. "I think we know one another fairly well."

"It was meant to be one night."

"Was it? Would you be leaving right now if we had a box of condoms and you weren't exhausted?"

Was she trying to kill him with lust? He could picture that all too clearly. "Hell no."

"Then we have nothing to worry about."

"Lust wanes. What then?"

"I don't plan on it waning any time soon. But I suppose you're asking about times like now, when we're exhausted."

Her comment deserved a smile, but he couldn't. He couldn't imagine being sated by her any time soon either.

"Then we do what every other couple does," she finished.

Michael didn't trust his feelings. He couldn't give Ileana the trump card she needed to win against her father. But he could give them a chance.

"We have to keep our relationship secret for now." He held up his hand to forestall her protest. "Until we get to know one another out of bed."

"Won't that be hard to do if we can't go anywhere together?"

"Miami's a big city. There's lots to do, plenty of places where we won't risk running into people we know."

"I won't hide for long, Michael. I'm not ashamed to be with you."

Part of his heart flooded with warmth. He slid his arms around her. She did the same and leaned her head against his shoulder.

"I'm not ashamed of you, Ileana. You're beautiful, intelligent, passionate, and caring." For each word, Michael placed a kiss on her face. "You're everything a man could want."

She raised her head and looked at him. "Even you?"

He swallowed his fears. "Even me. I want you."

"Then that's all that matters."

"I don't think we should have any more sleepovers over here."

Her face fell, and then she rallied with the determination he was beginning to love. Her chin came up. "I won't stop making love with you."

A smile kicked up the corner of his mouth. "I hadn't planned on it. How would you like to try out my bed?"

Her face lit. "Will there be condoms?"

He kissed her sassy mouth. "I'll pick some up today."

She squeezed his butt. "Get plenty."

"We'll still make love like we did last night, though, right?"

Ileana smiled. "I hear it's called foreplay."

Michael kissed her again. As usual, fire exploded between them. Her sheet slid down revealing her full breasts, but before they could get something else started, Michael broke away from her.

"I have to go to work."

"What hospital and what time tomorrow?" she demanded.

He hesitated. Tomorrow was going to be traumatic. But he really wanted her there. "8:00 A.M. at the Miami Medical Center."

"I'll be there."

Satisfaction blasted through him. He dressed under Ileana's proprietary scrutiny. Her approving gaze was like a touch. She checked the outer rooms of her apartment for relatives, and then it was time to leave. Momentous things had happened here in the past twelve hours. He was still reeling from some of them.

Michael took Ileana in his arms and kissed her soundly. She scanned the front yard for relatives and let him out the door.

"Michael."

He stopped and turned to look at her. Wrapped in her bed sheet with her hair tousled and her lips swollen from his kisses, she looked exactly what she was—a well-loved woman.

"I can't wait to see you again."

He smiled at her. "Me, too." And he knew he meant it.

• • •

Michael worked industriously all day updating himself on his business. The computer and his cell phone had made it easy to run his business from the road, but there were so many little things he'd ignored last week due to the press of time. Now, alone in his office, he caught up.

There had been no further incidents at any of his warehouses during the past week. Detective Washington had speculated it was because Michael had gone to the cops with his suspicions. Washington said he couldn't swear Miami PD was free of corrupt cops who'd leak the information to the perpetrators and make them lie low for awhile. But the major crimes unit was keeping an eye on businesses involved in the tourist trade anyway. Michael was just happy to stop receiving late-night calls from his security.

Thoughts of Ileana intruded all day. So did the fear that her father would find out about them before Michael was prepared to go public with their relationship. He'd given Esteban Calderon his oath, and he'd broken it. That didn't sit well on Michael's conscience. In his business, contracts gave peace of mind. He'd reneged on a verbal contract with the father of the woman he wanted with every fiber of his being. What a way to begin a relationship.

The box of condoms—party pack size—in his desk drawer distracted him as well. He got breathless thinking about having sex with Ileana. As the day wore on towards evening, his body's exhaustion gave way to fullness and aching. Ileana would not be disappointed by his performance. They hadn't made a date for tonight, but why wait?

His hand shook as he dialed her number. His stomach was tied up in knots. When she answered the phone, he blurted, "Ileana, it's Michael. Will you have dinner with me?"

"Sure. Where?"

"To tell you the truth, I bought condoms. So I'm only hungry for one thing. Can we please use them?"

Ileana laughed breathlessly. "I bought some too."

"Great minds think alike."

"I've got some enchiladas in the freezer. How about if I bring them over to your house so we'll have something to eat later?"

Michael had to swallow to moisten his dry mouth. "Sounds good." He gave her his address.

"Six o'clock?"

"I can't wait."

"You'd better plan to sleep over."

"Okay. I'll bring my condoms too."

When Michael hung up he found he was smiling. He was so lucky and he was going to get luckier. How had he found a woman like Ileana?

• • •

Ileana took a deep breath and walked into her parents' home. She could have called, but she needed her mother to be part of this conversation to give her unwitting support. Michael would be worried if he knew what she was going to do, but she could only keep so many secrets. Disappearing during a work day wasn't one of them.

"Ileana, we missed you at church," her mother exclaimed in Spanish. Yelina Alvarez Calderon was still a dark-haired beauty at fifty-five, despite her figure rounding with age. Her liquid brown eyes sparkled at her daughter.

Ileana and her mother exchanged kisses. "I went to mass yesterday," Ileana told her mother truthfully, although it was a wedding mass. "I need to discuss something with you and Papá."

Her mother ran a thumb down Ileana's cheek. "So serious. Your father is on the patio."

Ileana halted her mother by the kitchen island. "Mamá, you would never hide a serious health problem from me, would you? You know, for my own good?"

"*M'hija*, what is this talk? Your papá and I are healthy enough. You do not have to worry so about your papá's blood pressure. He will retire soon and feel much better. Do not be afraid."

"You'd tell me if you had cancer?"

"I do not have cancer. What has gotten into you? I am fine. Who has told you otherwise?"

"No one, Mamá. I needed to hear that you would tell me things even if they hurt me." Ileana hugged her mother. "I love you."

"I love you too, *m'hija*. Go see your father." Her mother picked up a paring knife and a red tomato.

"Why don't you come with me?" Ileana suggested.

Her mother peered at Ileana, then set down the knife and tomato, wiped her hands on a towel, and walked with Ileana to the patio.

Her father lay on a chaise lounge by the built-in swimming pool doing his doctor-imposed relaxation. He wore white slacks, a red shirt, and a beige straw hat.

He looked their way as they approached. "Ileana, are you staying for dinner?"

"No, Papá, I can't. I stopped by to discuss something with you." Ileana pulled up a lounger close to his and sat in it. Her mother sat next to her father.

"I need a few hours off tomorrow morning to go to the hospital."

Her mother gasped, her hand flew to her mouth. "Ileana, are you ill?"

"No, Mamá, it's not me. A friend of mine's mother has cancer—breast cancer—and she's having a radical mastectomy."

Her mother gasped again and crossed herself.

"It's her second one. Most of her children don't know. My friend feels all alone."

"It is good you should be with them. No one should be alone at a time like that. I do not understand the mother not telling all her children, though."

"I don't either, Mamá. I'm glad you agree."

Her father looked speculative. "Who is this friend?"

Ileana looked him in the eye. "Michael Ziffkin."

Her father stiffened.

"A male friend?" her mother asked, confusion in her voice.

"How much worse must it be for a son when his mother is ill and helpless?"

"Oh my yes," her mother agreed.

"He didn't want me to sit with him during the surgery. A man wants to appear brave. He doesn't want others to see his emotions."

"Yes, men are like that."

"He did not ask you to do this?" her father demanded.

"No, Papá. Do you object to me going?"

"*Chica*," her mother chided. "We do not object to you sitting with him during the surgery. Tell him our prayers are with him and his family."

"Thank you, Mamá. I knew it was the right thing to do." She rose.

"Ileana," her father stopped her. "Are you defying me?"

"Defying you, Papá? By doing what the priest tells us to do? To be charitable towards others, to help your fellow man, to comfort in time of need."

"You know that is not what I mean."

"If I am, are you going to punish me? Are you going to punish a man whose mother lies ill? Will you punish him while he watches her hair fall out from chemotherapy, while she grows thin with nausea from radiation? While he waits and worries if she will live?" Her father had paled. Her mother gripped his arm as tears dripped down her face. Ileana felt like crying herself.

"You raised me to be a better person than that." She hesitated. She loved her parents, despite what her father had done. He'd done it because he loved her. "Papá, thank you for telling me about your high blood pressure so that I can help you take steps to fight it. I'm glad you love me enough to want my support in your fight. And I know you love me enough to stand by me.

"I love you both."

She'd done what she could to protect Michael while he was vulnerable. Now she'd do what she could to make their relationship strong.

CHAPTER 18

Ileana had a condom in her hand when she knocked on Michael's door. As she raised her hand, the door was jerked open and Michael yanked her inside his condo. Without releasing her wrist, he slammed the door shut and crowded her back against it. She dropped her purse and overnighter on the floor.

Michael's face was tight with need as he pressed his body into hers, lowering his mouth for a searing kiss. Ileana wrapped her arms around him. His full erection jabbed her belly. A wild thrill ran through her.

His urgent hands burrowed under her sleeveless shirt, pushing her bra cups away from her breasts. Then his warm hands touched her aching flesh and began to create a new ache. She groaned into his mouth and pushed her breasts harder into his hands. He ground his erection into her.

Michael tasted of mint toothpaste. The scent of sinful cologne barely tickled Ileana's nose, and beneath that he was clean, fresh male.

He broke the kiss to murmur, "I can't wait. I have a condom."

She held up her hand. "Me too."

He wore navy boxers, so she simply tugged them down and he kicked out of them. He fumbled with her shorts zipper then gave a hard yank to lower them. She gave a shimmy and when they dropped, she kicked them aside.

Michael's fingers probed between her legs and entered her. She widened her stance to give him better access.

"You're tight. It's been a long time for you."

His finger moved in and out doing delicious things to her body. Her wetness soon made his movements easier and a second finger joined the first. He nibbled her neck and his free hand again found her breast to worry her nipple.

Ileana's body began to undulate against his finger thrusts. She managed to tear open the condom and fumbled getting it on him.

"Careful," he hissed. "I don't want to go off in your hands."

She felt like she might do that with his handling. His fingers thrust faster.

"There. Almost," he murmured.

A third finger joined the others. The sense of fullness left her aching for more.

"Come for me, Ileana," Michael urged, licking her neck.

Ileana could hardly prevent it from happening. Her vagina clenched around his thrusting fingers and then her orgasm took her to rapture. She moaned with pleasure.

Michael removed his fingers and dipped his knees. His penis pushed hard against her channel and slid into her. He drove hard. Ileana gasped at the unexpected pain, gave a little yelp, and then Michael plowed through her maidenhead and into the depths of her body.

He stilled, shaking. "Ileana, you said you'd done this before."

"Not this."

Michael leaned his forehead against hers. "You should have said something. I hurt you."

"I didn't think it would hurt." She gave a shaky laugh. "I'm almost thirty."

Michael began to ease out of her.

"Don't stop."

"I'm not."

Slowly he thrust back inside. There was no pain this time, only wonderful fullness. With several more thrusts an aching began.

"Michael," she begged.

"I know what you need."

He moved more forcefully. Ileana gripped his shoulders. She lifted a leg around his waist. Ah, there. He pounded into her body. She felt herself racing to the summit.

And then she was there. She screamed her release. Michael's shout echoed through the room. She felt his penis jerking inside her with his release.

They were both shaking. Her leg slipped from his hip to the floor. He eased from her body and leaned against her.

"That was phenomenal," he panted.

"Is it always this wonderful?"

Michael raised his head. "It's never been for me before. A virgin. But you had a *novio*."

"Pre-marital sex was forbidden. But they didn't tell us we couldn't do the rest."

He huffed a laugh then nuzzled into her neck. Her body still pulsed with aftershocks.

"You gave me something you never gave anyone else."

"I wanted to."

His body trembled. She understood. Hurt had come to the people he loved, which hurt him, making him fearful to love again. She held him and tried to give him what comfort she could. She couldn't give him certainties because there weren't any in life.

"How long until we can use the other condom?" she whispered.

"The time it takes to get to the bed," he answered.

. . .

Michael and Ileana got ready together the next morning. The intimacy of the past two nights made it less strange to share a bathroom; still Michael was surprised each time he turned to find Ileana beside him. His body was pleasantly numb, his passion burned up in the excesses of the night. They'd used four condoms. They'd also barely slept. Hopefully his exhaustion would dampen his emotions as well.

"You want anything to eat?" Ileana asked.

"I don't think I can. Maybe some coffee though."

She hugged him from behind and kissed his cheek. It made him feel better.

"I'm sleeping over tonight," she said.

He nodded. He didn't want to be alone.

Her multi-colored dress looked bright and vibrant. The silver bangle bracelets on her wrists jingled a merry melody. She exuded vitality from every pore. Michael tried to draw on her positive energy as they trod the somber hospital corridor.

They were directed to the cubicle where his mom was already being prepped for surgery. She wore a flowered surgical gown and a green cap. His dad sat in the chair beside her.

"Michael, honey. And Ileana." His mom was a little loopy from the sedative. "I'm so glad."

"Hi, Mom."

"Honey, I like her."

"I do too, Mom."

"She complements you."

Michael tried to distract her. "How are you feeling?"

"They gave me the feel good drugs. You should try it sometime. You're so serious. Always so serious."

His dad gave him a shrug, although his eyes were solemn.

Michael held his mom's hand over the gurney rail. "We'll be here when you wake up."

"Take care of your father."

"I will."

"And your brothers."

"Mom, nothing's going to happen to you."

She turned to his father. "I love you so much, Joe."

His father rose and approached the gurney, swallowing before he could speak. "I love you too, Janie. We've done this before. It's just like last time."

"I don't want to leave you, Joe. I'm going to have grandchildren. I still have things left to do."

"Mom, you're not going to die." The words ripped from Michael's soul.

"Promise me, Michael, you'll make up with your brothers. I can't stand to see this distance between you. It's hurting you. Promise me."

Michael swallowed and squeezed her hand. "I promise."

Ileana gripped his other hand.

"Mrs. Ziffkin. I'd like to pray with you if that's okay. Mr. Ziffkin, Michael?"

They joined hands and prayed for the surgeon's skill, the staff who'd take care of Mrs. Ziffkin, the oncologist, and for God's healing power.

God hadn't done much for Michael's family in the past few years. Michael wished he had Ileana's faith in His love. Maybe God would listen to her.

His parents kissed and then the hospital staff wheeled his mom off to surgery. Michael put an arm around his dad, took hold of Ileana's hand and walked them to the waiting room.

"Have you had anything to eat, Dad?" he asked.

His dad shook his head. "Couldn't. Besides, your mom wasn't allowed to eat. Seemed unfair for me to."

"I couldn't eat either. Are you hungry now?"

"Not yet. Maybe after your mother's in recovery." His father looked over at Ileana. "I'm glad you came with Michael."

"So am I."

"It's a source of comfort to have people who love you close by."

"My family believes so."

"The past few years have been difficult. After William died... well, there didn't seem to be anything Jane and I could do to bring the boys together again. It frustrated her and it hurt her. I wonder sometimes if the stress of it caused her cancer. You know they say stress lowers your immunity."

Guilt bit at Michael. Did his dad blame him? Did his mom?

"I'm sure that didn't cause the cancer," Ileana objected.

"Maybe not. Jane's been so happy since Richard and Charles came home. And now our grandchild is coming. It doesn't seem fair that the cancer returned."

"My father would agree with you. He has to step down from his company because of his high blood pressure. If not for it, he could have run Calderon for another fifteen or twenty years."

"We always think there'll be more time. William was only twenty-nine when he died."

Michael squeezed his dad's arm. "Mom's going to be all right, Dad."

His dad rubbed his forehead. "I can't help but wonder. We thought she was home free after the first operation. Are they going to have to keep cutting out parts of her each time it comes back? And what will repetitive bouts of chemo and radiation do to her?" He choked and then covered his face. His shoulders shook with sobs.

Michael drew his dad against him and hugged him tight. His throat and chest tightened. Ileana moved to his dad's other side and completed the circle around his father that Michael had begun. Michael ducked his head and let his own tears and fears loose. His burden had been nothing compared to his father's. His father was facing that thing that Michael feared most—losing someone he loved. And his father's love was so much deeper than anything Michael had ever experienced. How did his father do it?

Mr. Ziffkin's tears finally spent, he wiped his face on a white handkerchief he pulled from his pocket. "I'm sorry to fall apart like that."

"You love her," Ileana said, her voice husky. "We understand. I lost my *novio*, my nearly-betrothed, when I was seventeen. People said we were two halves of a whole. He completed me. When he was killed, I couldn't find a reason to go on without him. And yet I did. I walked the path Roberto had laid out for his life. I went to college in his place. I joined my father's company and did the job Roberto would have done. My family didn't understand. But I had to do it—for Roberto.

"One day not long ago I discovered I was alive again, that it was my life, not Roberto's. I had made it. That was the day I met your son."

Michael felt stripped raw. He refused to consider what her words meant.

His father nodded. "I felt that way when I met Jane. What I lacked, she had. She's so much more than I am. I feel like I've lived in the brilliance of the sun since I met her. I still feel giddy sometimes when she smiles at me. God gave me a precious gift the day I met her. I don't want to fail her."

"How can you? Hasn't she been happy having you for a husband?" Ileana responded.

"I think so. But I've been the lucky one."

"I think you're both lucky to have each other."

"Yeah." His father straightened. "Tell me more about yourself. You're Cuban, right?"

Ileana smiled with pride. "First generation American." She proceeded to tell his father about the Calderons and the Alvarezes. She talked about her siblings and their families, including her brother the doctor who made her parents so proud.

"My parents couldn't believe their good fortune to produce a doctor. We're a merchant family from generations back. But when Federico told Papá he wanted to be a doctor and heal the sick, there was no question of making him give that up. My distant cousin Roberto Herrara was to be my father's heir in Federico's place. He would become heir through his marriage to me. And our child would see that Calderon stayed in Calderon hands. It was arranged at my *quince*, my fifteenth birthday party. Papá was so pleased when Roberto and I fell in love.

"So my brother becoming a doctor opened the door of Calderon to me when Roberto died. My sisters are traditional Cuban wives. They stay at home and raise children. I'm the only one of my father's children in Calderon. If I perform better than my cousin Juan Carlos, Roberto's brother, I'll inherit Calderon."

"What if your father chooses your cousin over you?"

Ileana cocked her head. "I'd be sad to see Calderon pass out of my family's hands. But I'd still work for Calderon. I belong there."

"And where does Michael fit in?" his father asked.

"We're still working on that," Michael said.

Ileana gave him a smug, half-smile. Then she talked more about her family and her grandparents' escape from Cuba when her parents were children.

Her life was so different from Michael's. Traditions he could barely understand, like *quinces* and *novios*, defined her colorful personal history. Yet she'd broken out of the traditional female role and molded herself into the male Cuban role, something she couldn't have done in Cuba. She was Americanized, but not fully, immensely feminine, but with a searing intelligence and business acumen. She'd been limited solely by the fact of being contained in the Cuban community. Had she broken out, she would have been someone else entirely. He found himself thankful she was Cuban.

Her tales were so interesting that a step in the room finally alerted them to another's presence. They all turned towards the doorway, only to find not the surgeon, but Rick.

"What's going on here? Michael, your office said you were at the hospital. I was worried sick. I've combed this place for you. But you're not hurt. Dad? I want to know why you're all here."

Michael rose. He'd wanted his brother to share the load, but he found he had mixed feelings about Rick's presence.

"Tell him," Ileana said. "He has a right to know."

"He has enough to worry about with Analise," Mr. Ziffkin objected.

No, Ileana was right. Michael put his hand on his dad's shoulder. "Mom's having surgery. The cancer is back."

Rick collapsed into a chair. "What?"

Michael and his father explained everything to a white-faced Rick, who finally exploded, "You had no right to keep this from me! I came home. I came back to the family. I'm not a stranger anymore. I'm your *son*. I have just as much right as *him*." He jerked a thumb toward Michael.

Rage propelled Michael out of his seat once more. "Who stayed here and kept in touch with Mom and Dad? I did. I didn't run off to live my life somewhere else. I didn't give them the cold shoulder after Billy died…"

"No, you did that to me and Charlie. Are still doing it."

"I couldn't keep Billy in Miami where he was safe. Where his big brother could protect him. I couldn't keep any of you here. You just left. You left me, and you left Mom and Dad. They needed you, but they only had me. I needed you, too."

"Mom said you weren't to be bothered, not when you're getting ready for the baby."

Rick waved around the waiting room. "The baby will be fine. Does Charlie know?"

"No," their father answered. "He was getting married and now he's on his honeymoon."

"Cancer's a hell of a lot more important than a wedding or honeymoon, Dad," Rick declared.

"We didn't want to spoil his day."

"You were wrong. I'd have wanted to know. I bet Charlie will feel the same way when I tell him. I should have been here."

Ileana's quiet voice broke the silence. "Yes, you should have been here. Families stick together. Can you stay?"

"Hell yes. I need to call my captain and Analise. Oh, the doctor put her on bed rest. That's what I wanted to tell you."

"Do you need anything?" Michael asked. "A specialist? Does Analise need someone to take care of her at home?"

A small smile crossed Rick's face. "We trust her OB/GYN and she just needs to stay off her feet. But thanks for asking."

Some of Michael's bitterness thawed. "That's what brothers are for."

Rick pulled out his cell phone. "Excuse me. I have to make those calls."

"I hadn't considered his feelings," his dad reflected, staring down the hall after Rick. "We only wanted what was best for him."

"Tell him," Ileana urged.

"I will."

Rick returned and after awhile his father went to use the facilities. Ileana's eyes urged Michael towards Rick.

Michael groped for words to breach the gap with Rick. "I was angry at you. Because I had to carry the burden alone."

"But..."

Michael waved his brother to silence. "I was angry because you got to leave and I couldn't."

Rick signaled for Michael to continue when he stopped.

"Billy died, Mom got sick—it was like even God abandoned me. Then you and Charlie came back and you had everything. You both had someone." Michael rushed over that part. "Then Mom got sick again and they didn't want to burden you." Words clotted in his throat. "It was a heavy burden to carry alone. I had no one to talk to."

"I'm sorry, Michael."

Michael spun to face his father in the doorway. "I'm not complaining, Dad."

"No, you never complain. You're a good son." His father included Rick in his glance. "You're both good sons."

Rick stood. "I'm here for you—both of you—from now on. I never meant to be separate from this family. I'm sorry."

He looked at Michael and a heavy burden lifted from Michael's heart. Michael, his father, and Rick hugged. His mother was right. It was time to make up with his brothers.

CHAPTER 19

Michael envied his brothers' good fortune in love. Of the things Ileana had learned this morning, that amazed her the most. Yet he hadn't sought a relationship of his own. And it seemed for every two steps forward she took with him, they took one step backward.

He wanted something—her—but wouldn't allow himself to have it. A less confident woman might have walked away from him, given up on his moods, might have taken the moods personally when they weren't. A woman who didn't have the experience of true love that Ileana did might not recognize the rare connection she had with Michael. She'd had a soulmate once; she thought she may have found another. Michael was a complex man with layers of self-protection built up over the past few years. But she'd seen enough glimpses of the man behind the shields to know he was worth fighting for. Even if half the time she seemed to be fighting him.

Michael and Rick were talking. She sat beside Michael with her hand laced with his on his thigh. His father sat on her other side holding her other hand. A small, satisfied smile played on his lips as he watched his sons.

Ileana could grow to love this family, as different as they were from her own. If Michael would let her become a permanent part of his life. Convincing him would be difficult. His reticence wasn't based in logic but in emotion. But so long as they were together, there was hope. Which was good because she liked the picture she envisioned of them sharing a life together.

Quick steps approached the door. They all looked up to see a Hispanic man in green surgical scrubs. They rose to their feet.

"How is she, Dr. Ramos?" Michael's father asked.

"She's still asleep. She's in recovery. The nurse will come get you shortly." Dr. Ramos stepped forward and gripped Mr. Ziffkin's hand. "Joe, the surgery went well. I believe I got everything. I sent the tissue to the lab to be biopsied. I'll have the results tomorrow and we'll start chemotherapy later this week."

"Thank you, Dr. Ramos." There were tears in the older Ziffkin's eyes.

"Do you have everything you need, Dr. Ramos?" Michael asked. "I sold a lot of inventory so I'd have liquid capital, just in case."

"No, I don't need anything. I've arranged for your mother to have the private room as you asked. She'll also have a private duty nurse, although this hospital has a good reputation with patients."

"I want my mom to have whatever she needs."

"She will."

"Dr. Ramos, this is my younger son, Rick," Mr. Ziffkin waved at Rick.

The doctor shook hands with Rick. "Your mother has the best care possible. Your brother has seen to it." He nodded at them all and walked back the way he'd come.

Michael slapped his dad on the back. "The surgery went all right."

Although his dad smiled, tears stood in his eyes.

"You paid for all this?" Rick asked Michael.

"Only what Mom's insurance doesn't cover."

Ileana thought it was a lot more than Michael was telling.

Rick seemed to think so, too. "A private room, a private duty nurse—those cost money."

"I want Mom to be as comfortable as possible. Look, Rick, it's not a hardship for me. I live a simple life. I make enough money so she'll have what she needs."

Ileana wasn't sure Rick understood or appreciated what Michael had just admitted. But she did. She'd also caught what he'd said to the surgeon about selling inventory. Her heart filled with a warm feeling for him she'd only experienced once before in her life. It couldn't be love, not this soon, yet she'd known in an instant with Roberto.

A blonde woman in green scrubs appeared in the doorway. "Mr. Ziffkin?"

Michael's dad answered. "That's me."

"Would you like to see your wife for a few minutes?"

He smiled. "Oh, yes."

She looked around at the rest of them. "You'll be able to see her when she's fully awake. For now, it's just the spouse."

"Go ahead, Dad," Michael urged.

His dad followed the nurse down the hall.

When he was out of earshot, Rick turned to Michael. "I appreciate what you're doing for Mom and Dad."

Michael shrugged. "They're my parents."

"You've made sacrifices. You didn't have to."

"Yeah I did. I had to protect Mom. I couldn't let her die like Billy did. If the money made a difference between her living or dying, then I sure didn't need to spend it on me."

"It wasn't your fault Billy died, you know. He was an adult."

"You were all adults. That didn't stop me from being your big brother. That's never going to stop."

"I didn't feel like you were my big brother the past few years, even since I've been back," Rick said. There was hurt in his eyes.

Michael inhaled and exhaled a long, slow breath. "I didn't think you wanted to talk to me. The few times I spoke to you, you sounded so distant."

"I had my own guilt to deal with. I'm a cop. I should have been able to solve Billy's murder. But I couldn't. Until I met Analise, I thought all of you felt I should have done more."

"You weren't in homicide when he died. I never even thought about you finding his killer."

"Analise told me it's not all about me. And it's not all about you, either. I've put Billy to rest. Have you?"

Michael hooded his eyes. "I visit his grave regularly."

"That's not what I mean. Ileana, would you excuse us for a few minutes?"

Just when she was getting insight into Michael, his brother dragged him away.

• • •

When they were out of sight of the waiting room and other families, Rick turned to Michael. "Mom told me about your lack of relationships. I couldn't have been more surprised to see you with Ileana at your warehouse."

"I don't take every woman home to meet my parents."

"I think you've been pretty tight with Mom and Dad since Billy died. I think Mom would know what's going on with you."

"I'm a big boy. I don't share everything with my mother." Or anybody. "Is there a point to this?"

Rick ran a hand through his short dark hair. "What's your relationship with Ileana?"

"What business is that of yours?"

"I'm making it my business. I saw the way she looked at you just now with her heart in her eyes. But you don't look at her that way."

What was Rick talking about? Ileana wasn't in love with Michael. "We haven't been dating long."

"If you don't put Billy to rest, you're not going to get past the dating stage."

"I told you I put him to rest. He's not between me and Ileana."

"If you say so."

"I do. Now let's drop the subject."

Rick stared at him, the muscles in his jaw working. "Ileana seems like a decent woman. If you're not serious about her, you should break it off now before she gets hurt."

"Do you want me to stay angry at you?"

"No. I just want you to think." Rick massaged the back of his neck. "So what's happening with your case?"

"Nothing's happening. I talked to Detective Washington yesterday. They haven't heard anything from their contacts in organized crime nor have they spotted any suspicious activity in my industry. My business hasn't been bothered, and Ileana says there've been no break-ins on the retail end since we went to major crimes. All of us have increased security patrols. I hope whoever it was thought we were too much trouble."

"Don't relax until Washington tells you it's all clear." Rick looked down the corridor. "Dad's back. I'll go sit with him awhile. Go ahead and take a break."

As Rick walked away, Michael was tempted to find a coffee machine, maybe get a snack, or just go outside for a breath of Miami air, but before he could decide, a hand touched his arm.

"Michael?"

When he looked in her face, all he saw was concern...for him. It warmed him.

"What did your brother say to upset you?"

"I'm not upset." He gathered her close to him and whispered in her ear. "Let's take a break. Want to use a condom?"

She stared wide-eyed and interested at him. "Here?"

"There's a unisex bathroom down the hall. No one will know."

Ileana glanced down the hall then licked her lips. "Okay."

No one was looking. They slipped in unnoticed and locked the door. In moments they bared the essentials and Michael sheathed himself in a condom. He lifted Ileana's dress up. She raised a leg around his left hip, opening herself to him. He plunged inside where he belonged. Only him.

Ileana strangled a groan. They made love hard and fast. He tried not to thump her into the wall, but his mind whited out with pleasure toward the end. At least he remembered to groan into her neck. She bit her lip, her nails dug into his butt as her body spasmed around his.

He nuzzled her neck, kissing the spot where he'd accidentally marked her. To hell with what Rick said.

"You're all tense again," she noted.

"I don't like being here…in the hospital."

"I'm sure you don't."

He kissed her. She always seemed to understand. She could offer compassion and passion, comfort and joy, wisdom and beguiling innocence. Her mix was intoxicating.

They washed up and returned to his family. Michael was fairly certain he and Ileana had satisfied looks on their faces, which were a dead giveaway to what they'd been doing. Rick's raised eyebrow confirmed it. His father said nothing.

When they finally saw his mom settled in her private room, she was groggy, her smile loopily happy.

"Michael. Rick. My boys. If only Charlie were here instead of on his honeymoon."

"Mom, the surgery went fine," Michael reported.

"Always so serious now. I wish you'd smile more. And Rick, where's Analise?"

"At home, Mom. She's on bed rest."

"Oh." Her face sobered. "You shouldn't have come then. Your family needs you."

"You're my family, too. I need to be with you."

"Such wonderful boys. Ileana, aren't they wonderful?"

"Yes, Mrs. Ziffkin, you're very lucky to have them."

"You could have one of them yourself, if you wanted."

If his mother only knew.

Ileana squeezed Jane's hand. "Now that you're out of surgery, I need to go to work."

"I'm just going to go to sleep," she murmured. Her eyelids were already drooping.

Michael walked Ileana down to the elevator. They'd driven in separate cars so she could drive straight to Calderon. He took her in his arms.

"Thanks for coming. I'm glad you were here."

"I was happy to do it."

They kissed, a lingering promise.

"Later," she assured him.

"Come for dinner?" he asked as a family arrived to wait for the elevator.

"I'll be there."

"I'll grill fish," he offered.

"I don't know if I can sleep over," she whispered.

"Try," he begged into her ear.

They kissed again, and then he released her. He didn't want her to leave, but she had no real reason to stay. He was amazed—and grateful—she'd come today. He hadn't even realized he needed her here. Or that he'd needed her at all.

CHAPTER 20

"Castro is dying!" Ileana's young cousin squealed when Ileana walked into Calderon at nearly eleven o'clock. "Or dead already," her cousin added.

Ileana skidded to a stop in mid-step. "What?"

"It's on the news. Castro turned over power to his brother. He's dying. Some think he's dead already. This is wonderful news! *Tio* Esteban said to tell you to come to his office as soon as you arrive."

Ileana ran up the stairs, all professional decorum forgotten. Castro dead! It was what her grandparents and parents had wished for, for decades. All the exiles in Little Havana dreamed of the day. She could hardly believe it had come.

Her father's office door was open. She skidded around the corner and hung onto the jamb. Juan Carlos and several other staff members were there.

"Papá, is it true?" Ileana asked.

He looked up with such joy on his face—before he remembered to scowl at her—that her heart pounded with joy, too.

"We are going home!" he announced.

"Home?"

"To Cuba. Calderon is going home where it belongs. The island will be opened to tourists at last, and Calderon will serve their needs. We will have to import for awhile until we become self-sufficient."

"You'd leave America?"

"And you will, too. Our family, the other merchant families, and most of the residents of Little Havana. We have lived in exile long enough. It will be good to see home again."

Her nails dug into the door frame. "But it isn't *my* home."

"Of course it is. You are Cuban. You belong in Cuba. Your children will be born in our homeland. Cuban children. It is a wondrous day!"

"How soon?" asked her elderly uncle.

"If we are lucky, we will be home in a couple of months."

Her uncle crossed himself and wept with joy.

They were leaving. Ileana sank into a chair. She'd never thought she'd be separated from her parents and the rest of her family. Would her brother stay or go? Cuba probably needed good doctors. Would she be the only one who stayed?

Because she knew for certain she wasn't going. Cuba wasn't her home—America was.

"Will we sell our stores?" Juan Carlos asked.

"Sell the stores?" Ileana repeated.

"Having offshore interests might be good," her father agreed. "Especially while we're finding local sources of distribution."

"Wait," Ileana interrupted. "I could manage the American stores."

"You'll be in Cuba, *niña*."

"No, I won't." All the faces in the room turned to her, showing a range of emotions from disbelief to disgust, appalled to disdain. Her father's face was tight with temper.

"I was born in this country. I'm American," Ileana stated.

"You are Cuban, Ileana. Pure Cuban blood flows through your veins. We never intended to stay here. We were only waiting for Castro's regime to end. We are taking our children and grandchildren back where they belong. Our families, Ileana, and you are family."

She gritted her teeth in frustration as the people in the room talked about what they would take with them, what kind of transport they'd need, what their options were for selling the stores. They were all crazy. She wasn't going to live in Cuba.

As the day wore on, the phone rang off the hook. Everyone they knew wanted to see if they'd heard the news, to tell what they knew, and to see what the Calderons were doing, and when they planned to go.

Ileana wanted to scream. She was terrified that in his euphoria her father would do something rash like sell the stores.

She walked down the hall to Juan Carlos's office. He was closer to her age. Surely he was more sober and rational. She closed the door and sat in his spare chair.

"Are you going to Cuba?"

"I never really thought about it before. My parents talked of going home the same as yours did. But I've never been there."

Ileana leaned forward. "So you can talk some sense into my father."

But Juan Carlos shook his head. "*Tio* Esteban was born in Cuba, the same as my parents. He has every right to want to go home. It's been a long time in exile for them."

"But Calderon doesn't have to go with them, or at least not all of it."

"It's going to take a lot of capital to shift Calderon to Cuba. We're going to have to liquidate assets to get that capital."

She clenched her fists against the edge of his wooden desk. "We're a viable company, thriving in fact. It doesn't make sense to destroy what's growing in order to start from scratch."

"It's not your decision, or mine. It's *Tio* Esteban's company. He can do as he wishes."

"But he's stepping down. He could have named a successor prior to a move to Cuba. If it's me, I won't want to move the company."

"And if *Tio* Esteban knows that, he won't choose you."

"But you won't tell him, will you?"

Juan Carlos sighed. "You're blood, Ileana. My mother is your *suegra*, your *novio's* mother. I want the presidency, but I won't betray you to get it. Besides, I think your father will hold onto the reins until after we relocate."

Worse and worse.

"So if you want the presidency, you'll move to Cuba…just as I will," he told her.

"Do you want to go?"

"I'll do what I must."

"Please, tell me the truth," she begged.

Juan Carlos looked away. He had Roberto's profile. Through blood and his brother, Ileana was doubly tied to him. And to his mother, her *suegra*, her future mother-in-law.

Juan Carlos chose his words carefully. "I was born in this country. I'm an American citizen. We have freedom here the rest of the world just dreams about, including the people in Cuba. Their standard of living is lower than ours. This city, this country, is amazing. I love it here."

Ileana's heart soared with hope.

"But from my teens I worked at Calderon, and from the time Roberto died I knew I could be the heir. I've worked hard to learn all the facets of the business so I could be a good president. If I must move to Cuba to be the heir and the president, I will do so."

"I see. And the idea of retaining some of what we've built in the U.S.?"

"I believe I know *Tio* Esteban's mind on this. He wants to leave nothing behind here."

That included Ileana. She got the message. "Thanks for your candor."

"Ileana, don't fight your father on this. This is a dream come true for him."

And a nightmare for her.

•••

"He's planning to move Calderon to Cuba," Ileana told Michael as they lay together in his bed after their first urgent coupling.

Michael studied her face, her tense fists against the navy sheets. She'd called him on his cell phone earlier to tell him the news. And it was all over the TV. He'd caught it on CNN when he arrived home from the hospital. The news touched him as it did everyone in Miami, but not like it touched Ileana.

He had to know. "Will you move too?"

She turned anguished eyes to him. "I'm American!"

"So is your father. He's a naturalized citizen."

"Not in his heart, in any of their hearts. They've just been biding their time here. They've never truly assimilated. Look at Little Havana, look at its name. America is their mistress. They're going home to their wife."

"So you'll stay here?" A part of him was thrilled.

Ileana sat up and faced away. "If I want a chance to be president, I'll have to go. Juan Carlos hinted that my father wouldn't name a successor until we've relocated."

"What if he names your cousin? Will you return home?"

She faced him. "To what? Calderon won't be here. I'll have no job, no family. Most of my friends will emigrate."

Michael couldn't offer anything concrete like marriage. "You could work for Citadel. We could use someone with your skill and knowledge."

"I was raised at Calderon. It's in my blood. It should be my birthright."

"As Cuba is your birthright."

"No." Ileana said it quietly, with defiance. She rose and grabbed her dress, pulling it over her head. "I need my running clothes from my car. Is there a park nearby?"

"I'll go with you."

They donned tank tops, shorts, and running shoes. Ileana's movements were brisk and Michael was glad to see she had a well-used pair of Nikes. She was familiar with jogging. They stretched and then began a four-mile loop he ran at least three times a week.

Ileana ran fluidly like a deer. At first, her expression was intense, but after a few blocks, it relaxed. Michael wished he could do the same. He didn't want her to go, didn't want this time with her to end. But when she'd asked why she should stay, he hadn't said for him.

Rick's words replayed through his mind. Maybe Ileana leaving was the way for their relationship to end without her getting hurt. There was a whole new life awaiting her in Cuba. And men her father would approve of.

That thought irritated him and he kicked up the pace to try and outrun his jealousy. He should be relieved to let her go and tell her he hoped she got the presidency.

Hell, he'd have plenty of problems once he lost several of his biggest customers. He wouldn't have time to see Ileana if she stayed because he'd be working sixteen-hour days again. But if she left, Ileana's father was not only going to get to punish Michael through his business but personally, too, by forcing Ileana to Cuba.

If Michael said nothing, Ileana might go and solve one of his dilemmas. On the other hand, if he said he wanted her, it would put her in a dilemma of her own—her family or him, her company or him. That would be cruel. He cared enough about her to want her to achieve her dreams.

"You don't look like you're enjoying this," Ileana noted as they took a right turn to circle the park.

"I was thinking about the clients I'm going to lose. Some of them are irreplaceable."

Her gaze clashed with his. "Will you survive the exodus?"

"I don't know."

•••

Ileana held Michael's words close to her heart. She was sure he'd been playing the double entendre game with her.

Between the run, several bouts of lovemaking and the emotional day, she dropped off to sleep immediately within the circle of Michael's arms.

Deep in the night she was torn from a dream, her heart pounding, breath coming in gasps. She'd sensed Michael was in danger, then she'd heard gunfire. He'd jerked, and dropped, shouting her name. Had he been hit? Would he die of his wounds? She needed to know but the horror of it had woken her before the Sight could show her everything.

What could she do to stop this from happening?

CHAPTER 21

Ileana had to write down the dream before the details faded away. She slipped from under Michael's arm and felt her way out of his bedroom in the dark. As she walked in the direction of the kitchen, she hoped she wouldn't knock anything over or make noise loud enough to wake him. She was afraid she'd cling to him and babble incoherently in her fear.

Locating the light switch, she soon found a pad of paper and began to write what she remembered. The place he was standing looked vaguely familiar, although there were no signs on the white wooden building. Michael was wearing a navy suit with a white shirt, but he dressed that way nearly every work day. It was bright, probably sunny, so it had been during the day.

Would the problems someone was causing at his company escalate so that instead of targeting his business someone would target him? Or was that someone's intention all along? Michael thought he was being softened up for a protection scam. A perfect setup would be to frighten him, or worse, wound him. Unless that someone knew he'd gone to the police. Maybe now Michael was a liability instead of a prospect. Maybe someone planned to send a message to other targets—some form of, "Don't go to the cops."

Ileana shook with the cold that gripped her after one of her dreams. But she was also terrified for Michael. She didn't want anything to happen to him.

Although she wracked her memory, no other clues surfaced. She cursed herself. The Sight never showed her the same dream twice, so she'd have no opportunity to revisit the scene and pay attention.

But Michael had shouted her name. She had been there, too. Some of the buildings around Calderon were made of white wood. If he came to where she worked, that would explain some of the dream.

But he wouldn't come to Calderon. Their relationship was still a secret. They had no plans to see each other during the day. She stared out the back windows where moonlight reflected off the water. The threat wasn't immediate because it was dark outside now. Her last dream had given her nearly twenty-four hours' warning. She'd met Michael less than a day after dreaming he'd become her lover.

Michael planned to return to work tomorrow. He'd been away from the office for a week. She didn't think she could convince him to take another day off.

And with things so volatile at Calderon, she didn't believe she'd be able to take a day off to shadow him. But would he heed a warning from her? She had to try.

Ileana didn't think she'd be able to sleep any more tonight. If she was at her house, there would be plenty to do. But she wanted to be here in the morning to warn Michael, so she had to stay.

His kitchen was gleaming and modern. Michael had simple taste in food. He liked fresh food, easy preparation, usually healthy, often grilled. It was a man's kitchen, and yet she had no difficulty picturing herself here, making her mother's favorite Cuban recipes. Ileana didn't cook often herself, usually only on weekends, but when she did she liked to make quantities of food and freeze it.

The rest of the house lay in darkness. She could hear a clock ticking somewhere. Eventually, the regular ticking and the encroaching darkness soothed her nerves enough for her to try sleeping. She craved being in Michael's arms.

Ileana turned off the light and felt her way back to Michael's bed. He lay fire warm on the sheets, breathing softly. She'd lost her chill by now, so she slid in beside him and slowly snuggled her back up against him. He moved and his arm slipped around her. He exhaled into her hair and lay still once more.

She vowed to protect him, whatever the cost.

• • •

In the morning, Ileana told Michael her dream as they dressed to go to work.

"Was I hurt?"

"I don't know. I told you, I woke myself up."

"It was just a dream. You have a lot of worries on your mind right now. They manifested in your sleep."

"No. It was the Sight. You know I have it. I can tell the Sight from a regular dream. It's much more vivid."

"Ileana, I'm not a believer."

"But your sisters-in-law both have some special ability."

"I don't have to believe what they do just because they married my brothers."

Ileana hadn't considered he would doubt her. But she had to keep trying. "Will you promise to be especially careful today?"

"There's no reason."

She told him her suspicions from last night. "It could be the people who left the dead woman at your warehouse. They killed her. What's to keep them from coming after you?"

"My business hasn't been bothered since I involved the police. Whatever the cops are doing is working."

"Can't you do it because it will make me happy?"

Michael smiled suddenly and it transformed his face. "I'm all for pleasing you."

Ileana pinched his butt. "It's all about sex with you."

"Can you blame me? We're great together."

She wished he meant that another way. "Yes, we are. Dinner tonight?"

"I need to go to the hospital tonight."

"I'll go with you."

Michael hesitated. "All right. We'll go as soon as you get here. We can eat later."

Ileana kissed him long and hard before she left. "Be careful."

"I will."

• • •

Desiree walked into Michael's office soon after she arrived at work. "I've been watching the news. Cubans are talking about going home. We've got Cuban clients. Have you heard anything from them?"

"Yes. They're planning to emigrate. Calderon will go first. The others look to Calderon. I don't know if any of them will keep a presence here or not. Calderon probably won't."

She sat in his client chair. "How are we planning to react?"

"I'm sure clients will sell their businesses. We'll need to have the clients introduce us to the new buyers to make sure they continue to buy from us. And we'll need to find other new clients. I found some prospects on my last business trip I haven't had time to pursue."

Desiree frowned and shook her head. "It's crazy. They're Americans. Why would they want to leave the greatest country in the world?"

"The older Cubans weren't born here. They were forced from their homeland. They didn't leave willingly. They want to go home."

"You sound like you understand them."

Michael rubbed his face. He did understand wanting to go back to an earlier time and place. "Walk a mile in someone's shoes, they say." Which gave him an idea.

"Why don't you come with me to the Front Street warehouse? I want to check out the shipment of goods that just arrived. We can stop for lunch in Little Havana, get an idea how Cubans feel about Castro and Cuba. I'll see if one of our Cuban clients can meet us and provide a native guide, so to speak."

"That would be wonderful. Thanks, Michael. And maybe we can try to convince the client to stay."

Since he was going to invite Ileana to lunch, he knew Desiree didn't stand a chance, but he made a noncommittal sound.

Ileana accepted his invitation with alacrity and gave him directions to her favorite local eatery in Little Havana. He warned her he was bringing his assistant with him. Ileana responded by warning him they would more than likely run into people she knew there.

Miami traffic was unusually heavy for mid-morning. The traffic report cited Cuban celebrations.

"I think we're seeing exactly how Cubans feel about what happens in their homeland," Michael told Desiree.

"I've lived in Miami my whole life. I knew we had a large Cuban population, but I never thought much about them. I've only visited Little Havana once while I was in college."

"I think they want cultural separation." He'd found that out firsthand during Ileana's father's threatening visit.

The new goods from Indonesia proved to be mostly mundane. Tourists would buy them because they had Miami's name pasted on them, but Michael wanted something more from the goods he handled. The supplier's samples had led him to expect more.

Desiree echoed his thoughts. "Nothing exceptional in this lot."

"I know. I'm going to have to make a buying trip overseas." He always went alone, but Desiree had shown a natural aptitude for the business. Perhaps it was time she learned more of it.

"Could you leave Jamal and Tyrell for a couple of weeks?" Her son was only four.

Desiree's face lit with wonder and delight. "You'd take me with you?" She was an extraordinarily beautiful woman with an equally extraordinary intelligence. His friend was a lucky man.

"You've become a great asset to me, in case I haven't told you lately."

Her smile was smug. "You haven't. And thanks, for the compliment and the trip. I'll talk to Jamal tonight."

Michael watched her knowledgeable fingers touch the different items, while the look on her face assessed them. When he'd hired her as a favor to Jamal, he thought she'd simply take up the slack on the office duties he could no longer do. But her curiosity about the business had led her to delve deeper into business operations. One day soon he was going to have to discuss her aspirations and a bigger role for her.

Desiree displayed some of that knowledge in her next statement. "We may want to visit Malaysia, too. I've heard some good things about their products. I'll do some research."

"I'd like to spend a couple of days in Singapore to find some more exceptional pieces," he said.

"Singapore." Her look was wistful. "Jamal would love to see it."

"Maybe he can fly out at the end of our trip and the two of you could spend a few days together."

"That sounds wonderful. The logistics are something else, though. A sitter, the cost of airfare, him getting time off work." She sighed, seemingly daunted for the moment. Michael knew she'd rally because she was so upbeat.

"You have a passport, right?" he asked.

She nodded. "Jamal and I went to Mexico before Tyrell was born. I'll have to get it updated. How soon will I need it?"

Michael kept his personal life separate from business. He was the boss after all. But she might know some things from Jamal. And if they were going to spend several weeks together overseas, they'd have to talk about something other than work.

"I have some personal things going on right now. My mother." He waited.

"Jamal told me her cancer returned. I'm sorry."

"Thanks. She had surgery yesterday. Her second mastectomy. She'll start chemo soon. I don't want to leave until I know she's stable."

"I'll get started on my passport. It should be ready by the time you are."

"Good." And if the Calderons began shifting business and personnel to Cuba during that time, the timing couldn't be better for a buying trip. It would keep his mind occupied and keep him away from his home and his soon-to-be-single bed. Now that Rick was involved with their parents, Michael could make several buying trips. By this time next year he could be used to sleeping alone.

Yeah, right.

Their drive from the warehouse to the restaurant tested Michael's patience. Traffic was in near gridlock. He was sure most of the 650,000 Cubans in Miami were here in Little Havana. Crowds thronged the sidewalks waving two kinds of flags—one was American. He assumed the other was Cuban.

He called Ileana to warn her they might be late. She said she was in gridlock, too, and would wait for them if she arrived first.

Michael turned off the car's air conditioning and rolled down the windows. Desiree stared out hers in rapt curiosity. Horns honked a merry tune. People chanted in Spanish and English, "Free Cuba!" He heard firecrackers explode, and bottle rockets being shot off. On one corner, a group of young people were dancing.

"My God!" Desiree breathed.

They passed two separate TV crews, their microwave trucks transmitting the amazing scene to viewers. Michael glanced at his watch to see they were already thirty minutes late. He wondered if they would even find an empty table anywhere in Little Havana. Or a parking spot.

Luck or fortune must have guided Ileana's choice of restaurant. It was a whitewashed wooden building a block off the main street with a parking lot behind it where most revelers wouldn't look. Michael waited for crowds to cross the sidewalk before he could pull into the lot. It looked full, but he found an open spot. He unlocked his hands from the steering wheel with relief. Debating the wisdom of wearing his suit coat, he left it on in case the air conditioning was set too low.

As he escorted Desiree to the front door, Michael looked around for Ileana's silver Honda Civic. There were several gray cars, but he couldn't be sure if one was hers.

But when they stepped into the coolness of the building, Ileana stood up from a table and waved to them. Michael's body came alive at the sight of her. He couldn't believe it had only been this morning since he'd seen her.

Michael curbed the urge to kiss her in greeting, although it was difficult. He noted she was holding herself back as well. He settled for holding out his hand.

"Ileana. It's wonderful to see you." Would anyone notice if he kept hold of her hand? "I'd like you to meet my assistant, Desiree Carver. Desiree, Ileana Alvarez Calderon of the Calderon Consortium." Unfortunately, he had to release her hand so the two women could greet each other.

The brightly striped tablecloths echoed the striped awning out front. White ceiling fans circled wildly overhead. The place was packed with dark-haired Cubans talking with great excitement.

"I can't believe the celebration," Desiree exclaimed. "And a lot of the people we saw were too young to have emigrated from Cuba."

"It's like mass hysteria," Ileana agreed. "It's contagious. It's all anyone can talk about. I barely got any work done yesterday or today."

"We've lost a couple of hours ourselves," Michael said.

"How do you feel about moving to Cuba?" Desiree asked.

The look of pain on Ileana's face was quickly suppressed. "I don't want to go, but I have no choice."

"But you're an American citizen. You have a choice."

Ileana shook her head. "I'm Cuban. My allegiance is to my family. My duty is to Calderon."

"I don't mean to judge you, but that seems old-fashioned."

"Yes, it is. It was a hard adjustment for me when I went to college to live with non-Cubans, to hear thoughts so different from Cuban thoughts, from my family's thoughts. I'd lived my entire life within the walls of this place." She waved around her. "Talk about culture shock. But four years at Florida State could not sever my family ties and seven years at Calderon has only made my sense of duty deeper. And I'm more Americanized than my kin, so imagine how the others feel."

Michael's foot found her ankle under the table and rubbed gently. She smiled, but it was a shadow of her usual one.

"Are your family's American spouses moving, too?" Desiree asked.

"Cubans in this community rarely marry non-Cubans."

Desiree gaped. Michael avoided Ileana's gaze.

Desiree asked many more questions which Ileana answered patiently and with pride in her voice. Despite the problems, she loved what she was.

Eventually the talk turned to business and Desiree burbled about the upcoming buying trip.

"When are you going overseas?" Ileana asked.

"As soon as we can, although probably not sooner than a couple of weeks," Michael answered.

"We're going to Singapore, too. Can you imagine the exotic items we'll see? I'll have to remember to take enough money to buy Christmas presents for my family." Desiree touched Michael's wrist. "Back street bazaars. Maybe we can stay at a hotel off the beaten path so we have easier access to the local tradespeople." Her brown eyes glowed with excitement.

"I'd love to see Singapore," Ileana said a little wistfully. There was an odd note in her voice.

"I can't wait. I wish we could leave tomorrow." Desiree gave Michael a look of apology.

Lunch took much longer than Michael had expected. It was nearly three o'clock and they still had to fight the traffic to get back to the office.

Michael escorted the ladies outside, careful not to touch Ileana where Desiree might see. He was dying for a taste of Ileana's lips, but didn't know how he could accomplish that. This secretive business was not his way.

The crowd outside the restaurant had grown more boisterous. Loud salsa music and laughter assaulted his ears. He sidestepped a pair of what smelled like drunken college-aged students, forced against the whitewashed wood of the building. This situation was going to degenerate if alcohol was being added to the mix.

Ileana's gaze followed the pair past Michael and widened. She opened her mouth.

But the gunshots drowned any sound she made.

"Ileana, get down!" Michael shouted. He threw himself at Desiree, who was closer to him. God, he couldn't reach Ileana!

CHAPTER 22

"Michael!" Ileana screamed as she dived for him, not caring about the bullets. It was exactly as she'd dreamed! When she'd seen him outlined against the white wooden building, she'd known danger was imminent.

The gunshots panicked the crowd of revelers around them. Screams pelted Ileana's ears from every side. Like dominoes tumbling, the surrounding crowd hit the deck in an outward spiraling wave. Car brakes screeched. The crash of two cars colliding started another round of screams.

"Michael!" Ileana crawled to him, heedless of her expensive slacks.

"Stay down, damn it!" he ordered.

Desiree lay on her side gasping, her face paling. As Michael turned her onto her back, Ileana saw the spreading scarlet stain on the woman's peach blouse.

Oh, God.

"Shit!" Michael hissed. "Desiree, lie still." He moved her hands away from the wound and blood spurted. "Christ!" He tore off his jacket and applied pressure to the wound.

This couldn't be happening!

"Call 9-1-1," Michael ordered through gritted teeth as he pressed down. Still the crimson stain spread alarmingly.

Ileana scrambled for her fallen purse and dug out her phone. Bystanders faced them, some still lying down, some sitting, the brave ones getting to their feet. Other people had phones in their hands, too.

She felt stupid and slow as she relayed their desperate need to the 9-1-1 operator. Desiree's limbs had grown lax, her lips alarmingly blue in the blazing August heat.

"Hold on Desiree. Damn it, hold on!" Michael ordered.

"What happened?" several people around them asked. The question rippled outward through the crowd.

"Tell Jamal," Desiree's whisper hissed in the air. She coughed and blood flecked the corner of her mouth. "I love him."

"You can tell him yourself." Michael's voice was harsh, his face a stone mask.

In the distance a siren wailed, then a second one. Ileana glanced around. Cars had come to a standstill. She pushed to her feet. The ambulance wouldn't be able to get through.

"Move these cars," she ordered the bystanders. People looked at her dumbly.

Ileana pushed people out of the way until she stood at the edge of the sidewalk. "Move your cars!" she shouted. "We need an ambulance. Get out of the way!" She waved her arms in the direction away from the sirens.

"Get out of the way!" she snarled at one driver who was rubbernecking.

The sirens weren't coming any closer. They probably couldn't get through. Ileana faced that direction. "Clear the sidewalk," she yelled to the crowd, signaling them off. "Clear a path! Pass the word. Clear a path!"

As word passed through the crowd, people stepped off the sidewalk into the snarled traffic. Was she only making matters worse? She wrung her hands. She had to do something.

"Please, can anyone see if help is coming? Is anyone a doctor?" she shouted.

A middle-aged woman pushed through the crowd across the street. "I'm a registered nurse."

Ileana parted the people between her and the restaurant. They were all facing away from her, standing in a hushed circle around Michael and Desiree. When Ileana moved the last person in her way, with the nurse behind her, she stumbled to a halt. Michael knelt with Desiree's slack body clutched to his chest.

The nurse walked around them, knelt, and pressed two fingers against Desiree's neck.

Ileana didn't think she breathed as she waited. Then the nurse shook her dark head and bowed it. "I'm sorry."

No! Ileana had only left them for a few minutes. Desiree couldn't be dead. Nooooooo. It was a silent scream in her head. She stumbled to Michael's side, her only thought now to be with him. He looked up when she touched him and the anguish in his eyes made her heart clench. She wrapped an arm around his shoulders, but instead of leaning his head against her, he turned his face away.

"I'm sorry," she told him.

"Make way!" a man shouted, and in moments a pair of EMTs and two uniformed policemen pushed through the circle.

The nurse stood and spoke to them in a hushed tone. One of the EMTs knelt where the nurse had. He searched for a pulse too. He, too, shook his head.

A young cop knelt too. "Sir, if you'll lay the lady down, we can help you."

"You can't help her now." Michael sounded choked.

"We need to find out what happened," the cop told him.

"Somebody killed her. Some damned idiot with a gun," Michael snarled.

"Sir, why don't you let go of her and tell me about the shooting."

Michael looked up at the young African-American police officer. "My brother works homicide. Rick Ziffkin. Call him. I don't care if it was an accident, it was still murder." He choked. "Oh God. I have to call her boyfriend and tell him what happened."

"That can wait," the cop advised, his voice gentle but firm.

The cop and both EMTs peeled Michael's bloody fingers from Desiree. Then the cop pulled Michael to the side. His white dress shirt was covered in wet scarlet splotches. He had a bloody smear across one cheek to his temple where he must have swiped his face.

After the cops moved him away from Desiree, he didn't look at Ileana or hold her hand. He was shutting her out, or walling himself in.

• • •

As the cops questioned him, Michael's mind swayed from how close that shooter had come to killing Ileana instead of Desiree, to the horrible knowledge that Desiree was dead. God was a vicious god, turning His wrath on the people closest to Michael, punishing him over and over. Michael would not pray now for Desiree. He would not make obeisance to a God who was this cruel.

It could have been Ileana. Michael broke out in a cold sweat. He lost what the cop was saying. Wouldn't that be ironic—if she'd been killed by her own people? He was emotionally shaky.

"Mr. Ziffkin, do you want to sit down?" Robinson was the young cop's name, Michael remembered.

Michael shook his head. He was afraid if he sat he wouldn't be able to get back up again. He was afraid he'd cry like a baby.

"So you didn't see anyone with a gun, didn't actually see it happen?" Robinson asked.

"No. There were so many people, so much noise." They should never have come to Little Havana. Once they'd realized what was happening down here, they should have stayed away. "It's my fault. I should not have come here, not today. It's my fault she's dead." Jamal might never speak to him again. God, Jamal.

Ileana gasped. "Michael, it's not your fault."

"I need to call her boyfriend." The blood drying on Michael's palms was sticky and uncomfortable in the muggy heat.

"We'll need to notify her next of kin."

Michael flinched. "That would be her son. He's four. She lives... lived...with Jamal Blake. He's my best friend."

He heard Ileana inhale, a surprised sound.

"All right. Make the call while we wait for your brother. Although you understand this isn't his jurisdiction."

Michael nodded. He didn't care. The cops could fight it out amongst themselves. He couldn't take anymore right now. He just needed a familiar face near him. One who could take care of himself.

Michael found his discarded jacket and fumbled through the pocket for his phone. His fingers shook as he speed dialed his friend. God, what should he say?

"Michael, man, what's up?" Jamal sounded happy.

That only made what Michael had to say harder. "Jamal." He choked. He couldn't get the words out."

"What is it?" His friend's tone was sharp. "What's wrong? Is it your mom?"

Michael was aware of Ileana watching him in concern, as his valued control slipped where she could see it. "Jamal, there's been a shooting. Jamal, it's Desiree."

"Is she all right?" his friend demanded sharply.

"No." The word sighed out.

"How bad?"

"She's dead. Bled to death before the EMTs got there." Michael knew he should pretty it up, but the horror of it slipped out.

"No!" Jamal gave an anguished cry. "Where are you?"

"Little Havana."

"I'll be right there."

"Jamal, you can't get in here. That's why the EMTs couldn't get through. Thousands of Cubans have jammed Little Havana. Traffic's not moving. Don't come down here, man."

"I've got to see her!"

"Wait!" Michael held the phone away from his face. "Where should he go?" he asked Robinson.

"The downtown morgue on Seventh Street."

Michael repeated the information to his friend.

"The morgue," Jamal sobbed. "Oh God. It's true."

"I'll be there as soon as I'm done with the cops. You won't be alone."

After a minute of hoarse sobs, Jamal demanded. "What the hell were you doing in Little Havana?"

Making one of the worst mistakes of his life. "Meeting a client."

"Didn't you see what was going on down there? What the hell were you thinking to drag Desiree into something like that? I thought you were my friend!"

Michael took that last shot in the solar plexus. "I'm sorry."

"You bastard." Jamal sobbed and hung up.

Michael felt like crap.

"It wasn't your fault," Ileana repeated.

"Like hell it wasn't," he snarled and looked at her for the first time. The sympathy in her face poured over him like acid. He didn't deserve her sympathy. He deserved a horsewhipping. Jamal had entrusted Michael with the love of his life, and now she was dead. For the second time in his life, Michael had failed to protect someone.

It could have been Ileana.

They stood in the clinging afternoon humidity while the police went over and over the events until Michael thought he would scream with frustration.

Finally he snapped, "Does Desiree have to lie here in this heat?" He nodded towards the blanket-covered body. The EMTs had already left.

"Just until Homicide gets here," Robinson said.

"You know damn well in this mess it could be an hour."

"We know you're upset, Mr. Ziffkin. Just try to be patient and remain calm. Would you like something cold to drink?"

"Yeah." He hunched his shoulders and told himself this wasn't their fault. No, he knew whose fault it was.

As he took the cold Coke Robinson's Hispanic partner brought him and Ileana from the restaurant, Michael idly noted dirt on Ileana's slacks. The knee had a tear in it. When had that happened? He noticed her pallor.

"Why don't you sit down?" he told her.

"When you do," she responded.

Michael turned away. She was using the compassion he so admired in her against him. She didn't realize it wouldn't work this time. She was too big a risk now. It could have been her. If he allowed her into his life, one day it would be her. And he'd be like Jamal, wishing he'd died instead of Desiree.

It seemed like forever before someone laid a hand on Michael's shoulder.

"Michael." Rick's voice nearly drove him to his knees.

Michael turned. Rick's face held compassion and concern.

Something shook loose inside of Michael. "Someone killed my assistant, Desiree, just like someone killed Billy. There were hundreds of people around us. It could have been anyone."

Rick slid his arm around Michael's shoulders. This wasn't right. Michael was the big brother, not Rick. But they'd stood like this many times in their lives.

"Is any of that blood on you yours?" Rick asked.

Michael shook his head. "No. It's hers. I couldn't stop the bleeding. I couldn't save her."

"It happens sometimes. Arteries are like that."

"It was my fault. I brought her down here into this mess."

"You didn't know someone would have a gun."

"There's always some nut with a gun. They're everywhere."

"And you're sure it was a celebrant?"

Michael frowned at his brother. "What?"

"You're sure it wasn't that other matter?"

Michael went ice cold. He turned to face Rick fully. "You mean I was the target?" His lips felt numb.

"Maybe. Or if they know Desiree worked with you, maybe she was the target. Or there's another possibility." Rick looked pointedly at Ileana, whose eyes widened.

Michael felt like he'd been sucker punched. He could barely catch his breath. He doubled over.

"Michael!" Both Rick and Ileana called his name.

Oh God, oh God. It could have been Ileana. "Get her out of here! Get her away from me."

"You might have been the target," Rick said.

"You don't know that."

"She's a witness the same as you. Until we process the scene, we need her here."

Michael straightened, his eyes darting around. The crowd was still thick. He, Ileana, Rick, and the patrol officers stood in a small pocket by themselves—perfect targets.

"Jesus, Rick, we're sitting ducks out here!"

"I don't think anybody is stupid enough to fire into three police officers to get either of you. If that's what happened here."

"Are you trying to give me a heart attack?"

"I'm sorry. I didn't mean to spook you. I just wanted to make sure you were aware of all the scenarios."

"I'm aware now." Hyper aware, in fact. Michael felt jittery waiting for the sound of another gunshot. And this one might have Ileana's name on it.

CHAPTER 23

No gunshots disturbed the investigation, despite Michael's taut nerves. The homicide detectives assigned to the closest precinct arrived, and together with Rick, went over the chain of events. Michael and Ileana were questioned again, and to Michael's great relief, Desiree's body was sent to the morgue.

He was walking with Rick towards the parking lot when Ileana waylaid him. "Michael, we need to talk."

"I can't. I have to meet Desiree's boyfriend at the morgue."

"I'll go with you."

"No. Jamal doesn't know you. It's going to be hard enough for him without a stranger being present."

"I thought you might need me."

"That's not necessary."

Ileana looked pointedly at Rick, and Rick stepped out of hearing range. "I'll come over later, then."

"No, I don't know how long I'll be with Jamal."

Ileana got that familiar determined look on her face. "I'm not going to let you throw away what we have because you're afraid."

"It could have been you." The words were tortured.

Ileana flinched. *But it wasn't.* The words died on her lips. That didn't matter to Michael right now.

"You're going to have to talk to me sometime."

No, it was better this way. He headed for his car.

Rick rejoined him, glancing over his shoulder at Ileana. "What the hell are you doing, bro? Yesterday you were all over each other. Today you're giving her the brush-off?"

"Stay out of it."

"I can't. It's the Billy thing all over again, isn't it? Somebody you cared about died and you're pushing everyone else away."

"Shut up, Rick."

"You're making a mistake. You shouldn't be making important decisions when you're shook up."

"I'm thinking pretty damn clear right now."

"You're not. You saw somebody you cared about killed today. You felt threatened yourself. You were afraid for the woman you love."

"I don't love her," Michael denied instantly.

"Sorry. It looked like it to me."

"We're not in love." Couldn't be. Mustn't be, for her safety and his sanity.

"Okay then. The woman you're sleeping with. You were and still are afraid for her. Pushing her away is the wrong thing to do."

"It's the only thing to do."

"You've always been bullheaded. Now you're just being stupid." Rick stormed off.

Michael slid into his hot car. With the traffic snarl still out front, he had no hope of keeping cool. What Rick said didn't help either. Anger smoldered inside him. His brother didn't understand. Billy's death had ripped a huge hole inside Michael. Now Desiree's death had blasted another one. He couldn't take another savaging.

By the time he reached the morgue, he wondered if Jamal would still be there. But Michael was directed to a room where his friend stood beside Desiree's body. Michael hesitated at the door. Jamal needed time alone.

But his friend looked up from his lover's body. Tears traced his lean cheeks and welled in his brown eyes. His short dreadlocks were tied back from his handsome African-American face. His straight proud nose and full lips had made plenty of women chase him in their college days together. But in the past half-decade, he'd seen only one woman.

Michael went to his friend and slid an arm around Jamal's shoulders.

Jamal scrubbed at his face. "How did this happen?"

Michael told him what he knew, including why they'd been there. He noted Jamal's attention riveted to the dried blood on Michael's hands as he spoke. Jamal's shoulders shook with sobs.

Michael ended with, "I'm so sorry."

Jamal stroked Desiree's forearm. "I want to be angry at you for taking her into that mess. I want to hate you for taking away the best thing in my life."

"You should be angry at me. This was my fault."

"No. You didn't shoot the gun. It's not your fault."

"She depended on me to make intelligent decisions. I didn't."

"She was so happy working for you. It's like she came alive with the work. She wanted to know everything about import-export."

"She was very good at her job. I was going to promote her."

Jamal looked at Michael. "She would have liked that. We were talking about trying for another baby."

"I was going to take her on my next buying trip overseas and to Singapore."

Jamal frowned as he stared at Desiree. "She didn't tell me that."

"We just talked about it today."

"So you were running off with my girlfriend."

"She wanted you to join her in Singapore. Maybe to start work on making that new baby." And Michael had ruined it for them.

"I would have liked that." Jamal choked. "She filled up so much space in my life. How can I go on with the emptiness where she used to be?"

Michael held his friend while he cried. Michael felt horrible for doing this to him.

Jamal wiped his eyes. "I have to tell Tyrell."

"Where is he?"

"At the sitter's. I called her and she said she'd keep him as long as necessary." Jamal caressed Desiree's mussed curls. "I don't even know what arrangements to make. We never talked about something like this happening. Why would we?"

"Maybe do for her whatever you want for yourself."

"I think...burial...for Tyrell's sake. So he has a place to go to remember her. Maybe for me, too." Tears leaked slowly down Jamal's face.

"That sounds good. You'll want a service of some kind, won't you?"

"Her mom'll want one. We'll talk about it when she gets here." Jamal drew in a gasping breath. "Yeah. To celebrate her life, what we loved about her."

That philosophy differed from Michael's. Weren't funerals to mourn what you'd lost? "You're going to celebrate?"

"I don't want to stand around and be sad. Desiree would have hated that. Sure, I feel like my heart has been ripped out of my chest, but that's because the love we shared was so wonderful, so life-affirming. I was blessed to have her for as long as I did."

Michael couldn't understand. "But it hurts so much. How can you stand it?"

"I can bear it because I have those other memories—the good ones. She filled every corner of my life with joy and wonder. She made me a bigger man because she filled those spaces. I want to shout it to the world what she was to me. I wouldn't trade the time we had together just because it hurts now. Yeah, I wish her back again. But I wouldn't wish I'd never met her."

Jamal smiled tearfully at Desiree. He laid his hand on her cheek, bent and kissed her lips. "I love you, girl. I love you."

He let Michael lead him away to the lobby where they waited for Desiree's mother to arrive.

"I should have married her," Jamal murmured out of the blue. "Then I would have been her next of kin. We lived together four years, and yet I have no rights with her."

"You said you wanted to live together first, to make sure it lasted."

"That was years ago. Obviously it lasted. I should have asked her. Hell, we were gonna have a second child. Of course I should have asked her. We couldn't have been more committed."

"We all have regrets."

"Yeah, at least I had someone to love. You haven't even had that."

Michael didn't have to reply, because an African-American woman who looked a lot like Desiree came through the doors and began to cry as she spotted Jamal. He went to her immediately and they held one another tightly.

Family, Michael thought. Jamal didn't need to be married to Desiree to be a part of her family. They would draw together now, including Jamal in their mourning and celebration. They would give one another strength.

It was an amazing revelation. Ileana had said something similar. Had Michael and his brothers done the wrong thing by pulling away from each other to mourn privately? Was pain shared really pain halved? Could they have celebrated Billy's time with them instead of being frozen at the moment of his death, unable to move past it?

Michael felt shaken inside. He was too afraid of more pain to reach out again, but Ileana had already gotten under his skin. He didn't even have to stretch far to reach her. How badly did he want Ileana in his life? Badly enough to go through the pain he'd felt when Billy was killed—only much worse? The thought made Michael feel physically ill. To see Ileana on a metal gurney like the one Desiree was on...God, he couldn't do it.

But what if she didn't die young and tragically? What if she lived to be an old woman with white hair and great grandchildren—his and hers?

There were no guarantees in life.

And would she stay if he asked her to? Could she give up her life's dream and her family for him?

Could he risk it?

• • •

Ileana returned to the safety and familiarity of her family. She didn't understand Michael's response to pain. The rest of the Cuban population seemed to have gone mad, but in her parents' house she found the Calderons celebrating dinner quietly.

"Ileana, where have you been all day?" her father demanded as she entered the kitchen. "There was much to do at work. I do not like your going off during the day."

Her mother got a good look at Ileana's torn and dirty slacks. She gasped. "Ileana, what happened to you?"

"There was a shooting in Little Havana. I'd gone there for lunch."

"We heard about it. Thank God you were not hurt." Her mother crossed herself.

Ileana was enveloped in motherly concern. Her mother pushed her into a chair and poured her a small amount of *café Cubano* in a glass. "Drink. You have had a shock."

Ileana sipped the fiery liquor.

"Your *abuela* heard it from a friend who heard it from her son that a black woman was killed." Her mother fluttered around Ileana, setting a plate with rice and beans in front of her.

"Her name was Desiree Carver. I was standing beside her."

"*Madre de Dios*! You could have been killed!"

The echo of Michael's words made Ileana flinch. "I know, Mamá. I had to give a statement to the police about what I'd seen."

"It could not have been a Cuban who shot her," her father said staunchly.

"Why not, Papá? You didn't see the frenzy down there, and nearly everyone I saw looked Cuban."

"Cubans are happy to be leaving this country. They would not shoot guns into a crowd and risk hurting family so close to our rescue."

"Papá, there are bad Cubans as well as good Cubans. You've got to stop this racist superiority. It's frowned upon in America."

"Then it is lucky we are going back home."

"No, Papá. I heard on the news just now that Castro simply had surgery. That's why he turned over power to his brother. He's not dying or dead."

"We have heard no such report," her father blustered.

Ileana pushed back her chair and strode to the nearest radio, which she knew would be programmed to a Cuban station. The announcer was saying, "The message, attributed to Castro, said, 'I'm sorry to have worried so many of my friends. I am in very good spirits, and the important thing is that everything is moving perfectly well in the country and will continue to do so.'"

"It is a lie! Castro is dead!" her father shouted.

"Not according to that."

"Castro's government is covering it up." Her father's face was beet red.

"Papá, I think you'd better resign yourself to staying in America."

"You have made no secret you want to stay in this country," he said with a note of censure.

"No, I haven't. This is my home."

"I think Ziffkin is the reason you want to stay."

"He's part of it," she admitted.

"I told you to stop seeing him."

"I'm sorry, Papá, but I can't. I dreamed of being with him."

Her mother gasped, her hand flying to her mouth.

Her father's face turned from red to purple. "You would lie to me about this? You would lie for him, a white man?"

Ileana stiffened. She felt her facial muscles harden. Hurt knotted her stomach around the food she'd eaten. "I would never lie about the Sight."

"No daughter of mine will be with a white man. I forbid it. That Ziffkin would even think to sully a pure Cuban makes me want to squash him like a bug."

Although Ileana didn't know if she'd be able to turn around Michael's thinking, still she had to protect him from her father's wrath. "You will not touch Michael."

"So it is Michael now. You have been seeing him behind my back, defying me."

Ileana lifted her chin and squarely faced her father. "I love him."

"Love," her father exploded. "What do you know about love? You are a child."

"I'm almost thirty. I loved Roberto. I've watched you and Mamá, and *Abuelo* and *Abuela* Alvarez—wonderful examples of loving couples. I know what love is, Papá."

"I forbid it." Her father clutched his chest, huffing hard.

"Papá!" Ileana reached for him at the same time her mother did.

"Sit down, Esteban," her mother ordered.

Her father's chest heaved with each breath. Her mother fetched him a glass of water and thrust it in his hands.

"Drink," she told him firmly.

Ileana hovered, uncertain what to do. Her mother retrieved a prescription bottle from a kitchen cabinet and emptied a pill into her father's hand. He glared at her and she glared back. With sullen movements, he swallowed the pill.

Ileana gasped. "Is that nitroglycerin?"

Her father gave her a withering look.

"It's his blood pressure medicine," her mother replied with righteous indignation. "Your father has been working far too hard and I caught him eating take-out food the doctor has forbidden."

"Yelina," her father rebuked. "This is our private business."

"Bah," her mother responded. "I will not allow you to rob me of our life together because you will not obey the doctor. Our children will agree with me."

"Papá," Ileana chastised him. "The doctor told you how to live a full life."

"This is not about me, young woman. We were talking about your disobedience." His eyes got crafty. "If you want to be president of Calderon, you must give up Ziffkin."

The ultimatum hit Ileana like a sledgehammer. For a moment she couldn't breathe. Her mother drew an audible breath. Choose between the two things she wanted most—Michael or the presidency of Calderon. Ileana hadn't known her father could be cruel, but he had enlarged the company his father started and made it a thriving enterprise and he'd risen to the top of the Cuban merchant families. He must have some ruthlessness in him. Still, she was his daughter whom he proclaimed to love.

As she despaired of losing either of the things that defined her happiness, a disturbing thought intruded. Neither of those things was certain. If she gave up Calderon, she might never win Michael. His fears were deeply entrenched. And if she gave up any hope of winning Michael, gave in to his unspoken desire to stay out of his life, her father might still choose Juan Carlos as his heir. She owned neither of the prizes, but her father expected her to pay for them anyway.

He was watching her now with smug dark eyes, waiting to see if she would act as a dutiful Cuban daughter would. The Cuban papá was the head of his household—his word was law. Was she a dutiful Cuban daughter? She'd tried to be. He owed her for that.

"Who do you plan to promote, Papá?"

Her father looked momentarily startled, but soon regained his composure. "That is not at issue here."

"I think it is. You ask me to do something for you. What will you do in return?"

"You will not be president while you keep seeing Ziffkin."

"Will I be president?" she demanded.

"Ileana," his tone turned cajoling. "He is not our kind. He cannot make you happy, not when he will cause a break with your family."

A slow realization dawned on Ileana. Her father did not intend to promote her. "You intend to choose Juan Carlos, don't you?"

"Ileana, a woman's place is tending the home and raising the children. It's what you would have done for Roberto. It's our way."

She could barely deal with the hurt of betrayal. "Roberto died years ago, Papá, and my dreams of keeping a home for him died, too. I thought you knew that. I've learned how to earn my keep in the world. I've earned a place at Calderon."

"Only until you marry. Then your job is to take care of your husband and children."

"You expect me to throw away everything I've learned simply because I would marry? You think I went away to college for nothing?"

"I did not want you to go," he reminded her.

"Why did you bother to teach me your business, Papá?"

He opened his arms in mute appeal. "You seemed so far away after Roberto died. Your mother and I could not reach you. But then you came back from college and you had regained some of the fire you had before. You came alive again at Calderon. I wanted you to come all the way back to us so you could have the life you deserve—the husband, the children. But they are a Cuban husband and Cuban children, Ileana."

Ileana could go on as she was at Calderon, with no chance for advancement. Juan Carlos was her age—he could be president for the next fifty years. He'd bring his children into the business—his sons—and groom them as his successors just as his brother Roberto would have.

She would become *Tia* Ileana at Calderon, a spinster aunt. She did not foresee a time when she would meet a man who equaled Michael or Roberto, and she would not settle for less.

Her choice now seemed crystal clear. "You'll have my resignation on your desk tomorrow morning."

Her father frowned. "You are giving up Ziffkin?"

"No, I'm giving up Calderon. You've made it clear I don't belong there."

"But where will you go?" her mother asked in alarm.

"Michael Ziffkin offered me a position with his company..."

"No!" her father thundered. "I forbid it."

Ileana gave him a small, strained smile. "You lost the right to tell me where I can work, Papá. And when you think about hurting his business, know you'll hurt me too."

"But Ileana, he is not family," her mother protested.

Not yet. But Ileana would work on that. He couldn't avoid her at his own company. And right now, unfortunately, he had a job opening.

"The woman who died, Desiree Carver, she was Michael's assistant. Michael was standing closest to her when she was shot. She died in his arms. You should send your condolences to Citadel. A good businessman would. Oh, and she lived with Michael's best friend. Personal condolences seem to be in order, too. That's a Cuban philosophy."

And then she turned and walked out, heading towards the chance for a new life. All she had to face it with were her hope and her love.

CHAPTER 24

Michael hoped work would be his salvation, but he doubted it. Last evening with Jamal had scraped him raw, and Desiree's death played over and over in his mind. Nothing he'd tried had helped him sleep, and the little shuteye he'd managed to get had been filled with dreams where Desiree morphed into Ileana, her life draining away. He'd woken in a blind panic soaked in sweat.

Now, as he parked his car in the underground garage, he felt like a drowning man grabbing for a life preserver. Work had helped him since Billy died. It was his refuge, his escape, and his panacea. He turned off the car and sat flexing his hands on the steering wheel. Now his headquarters would echo with Desiree's absence. He'd probably have to face Nadine's tears. He didn't need that.

Maybe he should go work out of his warehouse like he used to. Maybe then he could lose himself in work. He reached for the key in the ignition.

A rap on his window startled him. A man he'd never seen before stood there dressed in a business suit. The dark-haired man was in his thirties, probably one of the building's tenants.

"Are you all right?" the man asked through the glass.

Michael lowered the window. "I'm fine."

"You're Michael Ziffkin, right? I came here to see you."

The man wasn't a tenant after all. How had he recognized Michael?

"My name's Pete Bosco. I'm in security. I've heard about your troubles. I have a pipeline into the police department."

"That's mighty convenient for someone in your business," Michael replied dryly.

Bosco smiled showing gleaming white teeth. "Yes it is."

"I'm afraid you've wasted a trip over, Mr. Bosco. I already employ a security firm."

"Clearly not as good as mine, Mr. Ziffkin."

"You're welcome to send me a price proposal. I don't know when I'll be able to look it over. My assistant died yesterday, so I'm swamped with work."

"My condolences on your loss. Who would have known she meant that much to your company."

Michael jerked. Had he heard Bosco right?

"Your company has vulnerabilities. I've studied it, you see. It's always good to know your target client."

Michael went cold all the way through. He glanced toward where the garage camera was.

Bosco followed his gaze. "The nearest security camera has had an unfortunate malfunction. Cheap equipment will do that. It's noted in my evaluation. I'd like to present my proposal in person, Mr. Ziffkin. I'm sure you'll find it irresistible."

Michael reached slowly for the ignition once more.

"Uh uh uh," Bosco scolded. A big ugly gun appeared in his hand. Michael had seen enough movies and television to recognize a silencer on the end of it. "You don't want to do that."

Michael slid his hand away from the key and rested it on the door.

"That's better. This was supposed to be a talk between businessmen. Now you've made me lower the tone. So let me tell you how it's going to be. Starting this week you're going to employ my firm to stop the break-ins that have been occurring. I can assure you I'll get instant results. And there won't be any more drug overdoses, not with my security at work. And best of all, I can assure the safety of all your other employees. It's unfortunate we weren't on the job yesterday. We could have prevented your assistant from being shot in that mob."

Jesus, Rick had been right. This man killed Desiree. Fear turned to molten hot anger. "You bastard! I've been to the police. I warned them I thought I'd be hit up for protection money."

"Yes you did. That wasn't very smart of you. But I'm a forgiving man. For an additional fee we can protect your family. Your mother's quite ill at the moment. We can place a guard right outside her hospital room at the Miami Medical Center."

Michael's helpless rage was joined by ice-cold fear. His mom! He'd do anything to protect his mom...but sell his soul to the devil? And if he said no and this thug got to his mom? Michael would never forgive himself.

But the cops would catch Bosco. Michael could give a detailed description now.

Bosco continued, "Your cop brother is lucky he's never been injured in the line of duty. Homicide detectives are going after people who've already killed once. Killing a second or a third time is so much easier."

Not Rick! Michael had lost one brother. He wouldn't lose another.

Bosco added, "And the woman you've been seeing, Ileana Alvarez Calderon. Such a beautiful woman and she lives all alone."

Rage like Michael had never experience before surged through him. He rammed the door open into Bosco with all his strength. The gun exploded, the discharge a soft percussive whine.

As Bosco stumbled backwards, Michael flung himself around the door and threw his weight against the thug. They tumbled to the concrete grappling for the gun. Another percussion whizzed past Michael's ear. He used all his strength to keep the gun from pointing at him.

He'd kill Bosco. Bosco had threatened his family, the people he loved. Michael had promised to protect them and he would, even if it meant giving up his own life. And Bosco had threatened Ileana.

Michael and Bosco battled in silence. Michael felt sweat beading his brow and hairline. He didn't want to die. He had so much still to live for—to see his mom well again, to make up with Charlie, to finish reconciling with Rick. Michael regretted the years he'd lost with his brothers. He regretted never falling in love, never marrying, not having an heir to give Citadel to, and for pushing Ileana away. God, he wanted to live! He wanted to see Ileana again and make it up to her.

"Freeze! Miami PD!" a man shouted. The click of guns being readied to fire sounded as loud as the shout.

Bosco froze and Michael used that moment to tear the gun from his hand. Then he rolled off the thug and looked up to see Rick and Detective Washington aiming guns at Bosco. Michael had never seen a more welcome sight.

"What are you doing here?" Michael asked his brother as he climbed to his feet.

Rick kept his gun pointed at Bosco as Washington cuffed the man.

"Saving your bacon, bro." Rick's voice hitched. "I was almost too late. Why didn't you just pay him?"

Michael shook his head. "I couldn't. He threatened Mom and you. I would have paid for Mom, but you...I had to protect you. And he threatened Ileana."

"Looks like I'm protecting you, big brother."

"Yeah, looks like."

"Better call in your team," Rick told Washington as the major crimes cop hauled Bosco to his feet.

"He killed Desiree," Michael reported. "Or ordered it done. Oh, and the other body was his work, too."

Washington handed Bosco to Rick and pulled out his cell phone. "Looks like you chose the wrong target this time."

"I'll be out within hours," Bosco bragged.

Rick's face hardened. "Don't bet on it."

Washington's team showed up within twenty minutes. Bosco was loaded into a squad car and hauled away to jail. Michael had given his statement to Washington and promised to do his part to convict Bosco. Since Washington and Rick had witnessed Bosco try to kill Michael, it wasn't just Michael's word against the gunman's.

Then it was only Michael and Rick.

"Thanks for saving my life," Michael said.

"You were doing a pretty good job of saving your own life."

"It was a stand-off. You made the difference."

"It was pretty dumb to jump a guy with a gun," Rick scolded, then admitted, "I almost had heart failure."

"He made me mad," Michael said.

"When he threatened Mom, me and Ileana," Rick guessed.

"Yeah," Michael admitted.

Rick wrapped an arm around Michael. "Thanks, bro."

"That's what big brothers do." Then Michael blurted. "I miss you. I'm sorry I was an unapproachable jerk."

"I miss you, too. Just try to keep me out of your life now."

CHAPTER 25

Michael's indecision was killing him. He sat at his desk toying with his pencil, unable to do the work his company desperately needed to survive. Three cups of coffee had only made him more jittery than the encounter with Bosco had, and hadn't cleared his sluggish brain to think. His eyes felt hot and scratchy from lack of sleep—Ileana's fault for teaching him the necessity of spooning.

He couldn't stop thinking about her and worrying about her. Bad things happened in an instant. The scene with Bosco had reinforced that to him. Yesterday's bullet could just have easily ripped through Ileana's beautiful chest as Desiree's. He couldn't stand to lose her.

But he already had. He'd pushed her away yesterday, told her there was no hope. Why didn't that thought disturb him as much as seeing her lying bleeding on the ground—like Billy, like Desiree?

Because she'd still be alive somewhere. In someone else's arms? His pencil snapped. Like bloody hell she would. She was his.

A moment of giddy exaltation was followed by one of being plummeted into icy water. *Michael loved her.* Rick was right. Michael would die for Ileana. She was one of the people he would have died to protect this morning.

He broke out in a cold sweat. What was he going to do about this love? He didn't want to hold her back from her heart's desire. He didn't want to experience the pain of a possible tragic death, yet he didn't want to spend another night alone in his bed.

To have her, he had to risk it all. Could he do it?

Hadn't he faced his regrets head-on in the parking garage this morning? And wasn't Ileana one of those regrets?

The intercom startled him, causing the halves of the pencil to fly from his hands.

"Michael?" Nadine sounded tentative and a bit nasal from crying.

"What is it?"

"Ileana Alvarez Calderon is here to see you."

Ileana. His heart nearly pounded out of his chest. He wasn't ready to see her, yet he couldn't wait another moment.

He swallowed and licked his dry lips. "Send her in."

Michael straightened his suit and ran a hand down his face. He was like a teenager waiting for his prom date. The door opened. He popped to his feet like toast from a toaster. And there she was, so beautiful she made his chest ache. So exotic with those slanted cat eyes she made other parts of him ache.

"Michael." The husky sound of his name slid up his spine like a loving caress.

Nadine stood behind Ileana, her mascara smudged from crying, so Michael couldn't pounce on Ileana like his horny body wanted to.

He cleared his throat. "Come in, Ileana. Thanks, Nadine. Would you hold my calls, please?"

"Sure, Michael."

Nadine shut the door, leaving Michael alone with the woman he loved. Ileana seemed stiffly formal in her caramel-colored two piece summer suit. Where did he begin?

Ileana beat him to it. "You said you could use a person like me at Citadel. I don't mean to belittle Desiree's death; however, I know you'll need to replace her, and, well, I need a job."

Confusion hit Michael. "Why do you need a job? What's wrong with the one you have at Calderon?"

"I resigned last night. I found out my father wasn't going to promote me."

"Did he believe Juan Carlos was the better candidate?"

"No, the better *man*. He wants me to get married, have babies, and be a housewife. He's wanted it all along. So I quit."

Michael felt dizzy with hope. "You don't want that?"

"Not the housewife part. So I was hoping for an interview. But I need to warn you, my father probably won't give me a reference."

Michael had to sit down. He waved Ileana to a seat and leaned against the desk. "I won't need references. But I need to know if there will be negative repercussions if I hire you."

Ileana shook her head. "I already thought of that. I told my Papá that punishing you would punish me. I don't believe you have to worry."

"Good." His nerves were easing. This felt right, her being his partner in all the facets of his life.

"I think I should warn you, though, I have serious designs on the boss."

Michael's tension unwound completely. A woman like Ileana came around once in a lifetime. A man shouldn't waste a minute of whatever time he had with her. He wouldn't regret it. "I see."

"You don't have any anti-fraternization policies, do you?"

"No, and if I did I'd have to rewrite them. You see, I intend to introduce some sexual excesses of my own."

Ileana's smile was like the sun coming out. "Excess implies unwanted. Your attention certainly isn't that."

Michael took two steps to her chair, lifted her up to him and kissed her hard. Before a second had passed, Ileana wrapped her arms around him and kissed him back. How had he ever thought he could live without this?

When they surfaced for air, they were both panting. Michael leaned his forehead against hers. "Will your family expect a large, Catholic wedding?"

Ileana's breath hitched. "Probably."

"That'll take months, won't it? Charlie's did."

She smiled beguilingly. "Probably."

"Then you're moving in with me today. I don't care what your family says."

"Okay." She kissed him. "Will you learn Spanish for me?"

"I'll do anything for you for as long as I have you."

But when Ileana tried to pull his head down for another kiss, Michael held back. "I know you can't promise not to die before we're old."

She sobered. "I wish I could. I wish you could promise me the same thing. But if we make the most of every moment we have together, then you'll never regret loving me. You do love me, don't you?"

"Of course I love you." Michael took her in his arms.

"Then there's no problem we can't overcome. Families, cultural differences, all of it. Because I love you, too."

EPILOGUE

Rick handed his infant daughter to his dad, who tucked her into the Snugli attached to his chest and cooed at her. Rick asked his wife, "You sure you're up to this, Analise?"

She looked up from where she knelt tying her tennis shoes. "We're not running it, we're walking."

"Stop fussing, Richard," his mother ordered. She adjusted the multi-colored scarf on her bald head and kissed the baby. "This is a day of celebration. Two months cancer free."

"Yeah, bro," Charlie mimicked, hugging his mom. "Stop fussing." Then he turned to Juliana and his smile faded. "You don't look so good. Do you need the soda crackers?"

Juliana's face turned from green to white. "No. I'm just going to sit down." And she slumped to the concrete next to Ileana. Charlie rushed to fan her.

Michael squeezed Ileana's waist. "You're feeling all right, aren't you?"

She smiled indulgently at him. "I'm fine. You're only asking because you like to brag that I'm pregnant."

"You're supposed to wait until after the wedding," Rick scolded them. He caressed his daughter's dark head.

"It wasn't my choice to wait eight months," Michael responded. "I would have eloped like you did." He and Ileana believed the baby would cross the cultural divide between him and the Calderons. And two more grandchildren were giving his mother something to focus on besides her recovery.

"Shh," Ileana hushed him. "Here comes Mamá. You know my being pregnant for the wedding is a sore spot with her."

Yelina Alvarez Calderon came bustling up to their group. "I am sorry to be late. I was putting a little more food on to cook."

She took Jane Ziffkin's hands and the two women kissed cheeks. They'd got on like a house on fire since the moment they'd been introduced at Michael and Ileana's engagement party.

"You're not cooking for an army, Yelina," Mrs. Ziffkin reminded her as she greeted Joe Ziffkin. "We're just family."

Yelina smiled as she looked over Mrs. Ziffkin's scarf. "You never know how much family will show up to eat. That scarf looks beautiful on you, Jane." She reached into her large purse and pulled out a long length of gorgeous dyed silk and handed it over. "But this will look even better. For your two-month anniversary."

"Oh, Yelina, it's beautiful. Thank you." They hugged and Michael's mom glanced around. "I thought you were bringing your sister."

Yelina lowered her voice. "She is putting on her walking shoes. She has never owned a pair before, so the going is slow. But I could not wait to see you, my daughter and my future son-in-law."

She turned to Michael with a disapproving look on her face. Michael's stomach clenched. Would the Calderons ever accept him?

"*Hola*, Mamá," he said in Spanish.

"Do not think to win me with your glib tongue when my Ileana will look ridiculous at her own wedding, being large with my grandchild." The last two words were smugly proud.

Then she smiled at Michael with the same pride. "Esteban and I have talked to the priest and he will allow us to move the ceremony ahead. The family will make the food and we will put a tent in our yard. We will be able to hold the wedding in a few weeks. It is clear you two belong together."

Ileana squealed. "Mamá, thank you!" She hugged her mother.

Michael gave Ileana a misty smile and hugged his future mother-in-law. "*Gracias*, Mamá."

Yelina hooked arms with Michael's mother. "We will shop, you and I. I will take you to the best places in Little Havana. We will find a gorgeous dress to wear with your new scarf. You will be beautiful for the wedding. And while we are shopping we will pick out things for our grandchild."

The two mothers smiled at one another.

Someone with a megaphone announced, "Welcome to the Susan G. Koman breast cancer walk. Everyone please take your places so we can get started."

Ileana's aunt, a chunky black-haired woman, broke through the crowd. "I am here!" She kissed and hugged everyone. "You heard we have moved up the wedding?"

"*Si, gracias*," Michael answered.

"*De nada*. It was Yelina's idea."

The walkers lined up. Michael and Ileana's families wore T-shirts with a big pink ribbon emblazoned on them. So did many other people in the crowd. Many were breast cancer survivors like his mom was. Many were living one day at a time, grateful for every moment they had together.

Michael had taken a page from their book and was doing the same.

The starting gun sounded, and they were off!

ABOUT THE AUTHOR

Multi-published author Shay Lacy lives in northwest Ohio with her photographer/graphic designer husband. She loves following the man of her dreams with a camera in hand and a pen and notebook in her backpack. Sensible secretary by day, romance author by night, when not lost in her imagination or reading a good book, she is likely researching her next book with a SWAT team ride-along or a visit to a DNA lab.

For more information about Shay or to see the books she's written, please visit her website at *www.shaylacy.com*.

More from This Author
(From *Secrets and Lies* by Shay Lacy)

Why would somebody steal a sculpture of a fertility god instead of buying Viagra? Private investigator Charlie Ziffkin had followed the thief's trail from Hollywood to Miami, proving this was no petty thief. His actions suggested he worked for a client—a rich one. Charlie needed to find out who had that kind of money for illegal activities. Who better to help him locate his client's fertility statue than a hooker? He hoped to get lucky on this street where they stood on every corner. He'd start with prostitutes and work his way up the food chain.

He smiled at the brunette in the barely-there mini as he approached.

The hooker's eyes glinted in the streetlight as her gaze ran over him from head to toe. "Hey, baby, I can make you feel real good." Up close, even the night and her heavy makeup couldn't conceal the wear and tear her lifestyle had caused.

"I'd like to feel good." Wasn't that the truth. Since his brother, Billy's, senseless murder two years ago, he hadn't felt anything but pain. "But what I need is information." So he could retrieve his client's property and get out of this town where he'd been born. Where Billy was buried. Why the hell had the thief come here, of all places?

The hooker's mascara-heavy lashes had been at half-mast as she'd leaned toward him. Now her eyes opened fully and filled with wariness. She took a step back. "I don't talk to cops."

"I'm not a cop. My name is Chaz. I'm out here from Hollywood for a few days looking to get connected, you know what I mean? I have lots of friends back home. I need a way to make them happy. You must know who to talk to when you want to have a large party. I'm sure you know all kinds of things, like who holds the money and power in this town. If I wanted something and I didn't want people asking a lot of questions, who would I talk to?"

"What do you do in Hollywood?"

"I'm a promoter."

Her suspicious gaze raked him. "You're mighty young."

"Age is meaningless if you can get things done. And I can."

"Baby, listen, if you're not interested in the merchandise, I need to make a living." She glanced around as though looking for another john.

"How much?"

Her sly gaze swung to his face. She ran her tongue slowly over her upper lip. "For you, good looking, thirty bucks."

Charlie pulled his wallet out of his suit jacket pocket and retrieved the money. He'd better not have to pay everybody for information on this job. His client had offered a hefty fee, but he'd only gotten a retainer upfront. He held the bills out toward her. As she reached for them with long purple fingernails, he said, "I need names."

"See Carlos at the Bottoms Up bar on Hialeah. He's there every night. He'll know who can help you." She snatched the money and stuffed it into her neon blue bra. A sultry smile lifted the corners of her red lips. "I can get rid of that tension you feel."

He was losing his acting ability if she could see that. He forced his muscles to relax and gave her a slow smile. "You've helped me already. Thanks. If you're ever in Hollywood . . ."

She shrugged. "Sure, baby." She strutted away on sparkling stilettos.

A blonde hooker lounged under the streetlight at the next corner. He fought the urge to jog toward her because he needed answers *now*. He couldn't linger in Miami. His parents and brother, Michael, whom he hadn't seen since Billy's funeral, lived here. He couldn't face them knowing he lived while Billy's body lie in a grave just miles from here. *Too close.*

Billy had been brilliant, with a PhD and a new job as a research scientist. He probably would have cured cancer if he'd lived. But a freak robbery turned murder had buried those dreams. The police thought it might have been somebody high on drugs or looking for money for their next fix. His murderer had never been caught.

Charlie, on the other hand, had been a mediocre student who'd only cared about one thing—acting. He'd lit out of Miami for Hollywood thinking he only had to arrive to fulfill his dreams. A dozen years later, success still eluded him. In professional terms, he was a failure.

But he was trying to right the wrong of living. He couldn't be Billy, couldn't take over where his brother's life had ended. But Charlie could succeed instead of fail. He could make life better for others, one case at a time. This was the biggest case he'd worked so far. Retrieving Hollywood producer Jordan Hessler's stolen relic would guarantee him referrals and success. He just had to find it and escape Miami before his past sucked him back in.

In the next block, a young Latina spoke to a john. She reminded him of his childhood and teenage sweetheart, Juliana Sanchez. She'd been his greatest supporter, participating in every dramatic endeavor he dreamed up. Rarely did a day pass when she wasn't playing pirates or detectives or space aliens with him and, as they got older, Romeo and Juliet. It had been just acting, until one day it wasn't acting anymore. Charlie didn't know when he'd fallen in love with her, somewhere around age fifteen. They'd had two years together where he'd had to hide how he felt from his best friend, afraid his heart would burst at the mere sight of her.

Then Juliana's mother died, and her father had sent her to live with her aunt until he could sell their house. Sergeant Sanchez had severed all contact between Juliana and Charlie. He should have taken his police revolver and killed Charlie; that would have been kinder. Thirteen years apart and, still, no woman had ever measured up to Juliana. He didn't think one ever would.

As far as he knew, she still lived here. For years after she'd been ripped from his arms and his life he'd wanted—needed—to run into her. But he couldn't see her like this. He was the walking dead. She deserved better than him.

Charlie drew on his acting skills. He forced his face to relax into a smile as he approached the blonde. He had to make the hooker feel safe so she'd provide the intel he needed.

. . .

"This bra is killing me," Juliana Sanchez muttered toward the microphone hidden in her long brown hair. In her opinion, push-up bras could be used as instruments of torture.

"It looks *fine* from here, sugar," Vice Detective Hector Muñoz drawled into her earpiece. "So fine."

She smiled toward where her protection watched from a white panel van down the street.

"Better hope her daddy doesn't catch her wearing that outfit," his partner, Detective Karl Polaris, retorted. "He's smart enough to put two and two together, and then he'll do worse than break us back to beat cops. I can't believe I let you talk me into this."

Juliana should be worried, too. If her dad, Police Captain Alejandro Sanchez, found out she was subbing for her friend in vice, he'd break her back to... Gee, what was worse than treating her like a teenager instead of a woman nearly thirty? She was stifling under his overprotectiveness. His behavior had been understandable after her mother was killed and Juliana was injured when a drunk driver had hit their car, but that was over a decade ago. Since then, he'd remarried and had two young sons who enjoyed more freedom than she did. They'd probably even get to be cops when they grew up, unlike her, who did medical transcription for a living. Damn it, she was an adult living on her own. When was he going to think of her as one?

She couldn't regret this act of defiance; after all, she was helping the police like he'd taught her to do. It wasn't her fault her dreams of being a police officer had gone up in smoke in that same accident when a head injury had awoken a psychic talent, making her unfit for police work. If only she'd ignored the strange tingling sensation that began at her fingertips and helped her "find" lost items—her father's keys, her aunt's missing shoe, her school friend who'd been abducted by an estranged parent—or learn things about an object when she held something connected to it. If she'd kept it to herself, she never would have learned she had the gift of psychometry.

It was too late now to keep her psychic gift secret. She helped the police where she could, normally the burglary department, with her father's blessing. But sometimes she had to sneak to do it. She lifted her chin and pulled her shoulders back, a mistake wearing this bra. Her nipples nearly popped out. Damn. And this barely-there skirt let the unseasonably cool Miami night air blow right up her crotch. Talk about a cold shower.

She tried to strut like the rest of the streetwalkers on this downtown strip of neon sidewalk. The five-inch silver stiletto heels were killing her, too. No wonder prostitutes were so eager to get flat on their backs.

Muffling a laugh, she gave a come-hither smile to a middle-aged balding man in a lightweight suit as he approached. He looked over her goods and kept on walking.

"Not in the mood, I guess," she said.

"Keep walking," Hector instructed. "There's some more prospects up ahead."

A dark-haired man was talking to a bleached blonde in a purple sequined mini-dress just a little ahead. The blonde looked eager—her feet probably hurt. The man was a smooth operator; Juliana could tell by the way he leaned toward her and ran a finger down her outer arm.

The blonde looked confused, then outraged, and then she smiled once more, sucked in by whatever the man said to soothe her. Maybe he was kinky but the blonde was willing for a price. Juliana got close enough to hear his smooth baritone and cajoling tone.

"My name is Chaz. I know people in the industry."

Juliana's steps faltered and she nearly fell over. *No! That name with that voice and that dark wavy hair—it couldn't be!*

But he turned his head, and his profile was as she remembered, except for the two-day stubble that hid his stubborn chin and slight dimple. He'd been seventeen and skinny when her father had sent her to live with her aunt. Now he was a man. And what a man. He'd filled out through the chest and shoulders. He looked sexy. Her heart pounded so hard at seeing him she could hardly think.

For most of her childhood she'd seen him daily. They'd acted out scenes from every play and movie he knew. She'd been Bonnie to his Clyde, Princess Leia to his Han Solo, Tonto to his Lone Ranger. He'd created worlds out of pure imagination, and taken her there with him. Anything had been possible by his side. She could be anything or anyone, and so could he.

And now he was picking up a hooker?

The thought startled her so badly his name leapt from her throat. "Charlie Ziffkin, what are you doing?"

Charlie whirled, and his summer blue gaze flew to her face. He looked like he'd been goosed. "Juliana?"

"Juliana!" echoed in her earpiece. "What are you doing?" Hector sounded like he was coming unhinged.

The blonde latched onto Charlie's arm. "Get lost, ho. He's taken." Her long nails were blood red against his dark sleeve.

"Keep your mind on business!" Hector demanded.

"Now, ladies," Charlie soothed as he slipped his arm from the blonde's grasp. "There's no need for name-calling. Trixie, I'm so sorry. Perhaps another time?" He always was a sweet talker.

Trixie gave Juliana a withering look and minced away on her five-inch spiked heels, working her scantily clad booty for all it was worth.

Then Juliana and Charlie were alone for the first time in thirteen years. Unexpected excitement pulsed through her body at his nearness. Her breaths shortened, and her heart raced. Tension pooled in her lower belly. She'd lusted after the skinny boy, but that paled compared to how the fully grown man made her feel. Now she knew what it felt like to make love. What might it be like to consummate what they'd started so long ago?

"Juliana, make a move," Karl prompted.

Charlie was getting an eyeful of her cleavage and everything else her outfit exposed. At last he looked her in the eyes again with dilated pupils. "You've grown up."

"So have you." She forced herself to take a step toward him, then another, until she could touch him. His heat rolled over her, making her sweat. Her pulse punched into overdrive. Her mouth dried. He would have been her first if her father hadn't stopped them.

She walked her fingers up the sleeve of his black suit jacket. He wore it with a high-collared maroon vest underneath, the collar standing up around his neck, and a black t-shirt under that. With stonewashed jeans, he looked trendy and sexy.

She licked her lips. "You look mighty fine, Charlie."

"I like what I see, too." His finger skimmed her bare arm, giving her goose bumps.

"Want to finish what we started all those years ago?"

His face lowered toward hers. His breath stirred the hair beside her face. He smelled like mint. "Do you need money, Juliana?"

"Everybody needs money." She gave him a steamy look. It wasn't hard.

"How much?"

"For fifty bucks I could ease that itch in your pants." She nodded to the sizable bulge in his jeans.

"Your father wouldn't stop us this time?"

Juliana winced inwardly. Her father wouldn't, but his minions would. "No," she purred. "We could go all the way."

Charlie stared at her with an intensity she couldn't define. She wished they were having this conversation under different circumstances. She dared not take too deep a breath for fear her heart would crack.

From inside his suit jacket he pulled out a black wallet. Juliana's smile felt ready to fracture. He handed the bills to her. It was like pushing through thick mud to reach him.

Their fingers touched. Despite him being a john, a thrill ran through her. She thought she saw sadness in his eyes, which made no sense. The moment seemed frozen. There was only Charlie and the shattering of a young girl's dream. He'd been her hero, even when he'd played the villain.

"Freeze, sleazebag!" Hector yelled, pointing his automatic at Charlie. She hadn't even heard him approach.

Karl materialized from behind Charlie, gun drawn. "Hands on the back of your head and lace your fingers together."

"Step away from him, Juliana," Hector ordered.

"Ah." A smile tugged at one side of Charlie's mouth, sexy and knowing. His blue eyes sparkled like sunlight off a tropical bay. "The family business." He put his hands on his head and interlaced his fingers.

Hector glared at him. "Shut up, scum."

"You're making a mistake." Was that laughter in Charlie's voice?

Karl was rough patting him down. Charlie never took his eyes off Juliana. Why did he think this was funny?

"You're under arrest for solicitation—" Hector began.

"You'd better look in my wallet," Charlie interrupted, even as Karl cuffed him.

Hector's eyebrows lifted. "You offering us a bribe?"

"No, I'm trying to save you some humiliation."

"He was always a good liar," Juliana informed the vice cops.

"Don't believe me then." Charlie shrugged. Hard to do with his hands cuffed behind him.

Hector reached into Charlie's jacket and pulled out his wallet. Flipping it open, he frowned. "You're a private investigator?"

Juliana's mouth fell open, but she recovered enough to say, "He is not. He's a Hollywood actor."

"Retired," Charlie said, smiling.

"It's not true," Juliana insisted.

"I'm on a case."

"You were trying to get laid."

He quirked a dark brow. "Do you think I have to pay women to sleep with me?"

Juliana closed her mouth with a snap. She couldn't imagine any woman saying no to him. "You offered me money for sex."

"I offered you money because I felt sorry for you. I thought something terrible must have happened for you to turn to prostitution. I did it for old time's sake."

Hector waved the wallet. "It doesn't matter what you say. Until this checks out, you're going to the station for booking."

"Ask that prostitute, Trixie, what I wanted from her," Charlie said.

All of them looked in the direction she'd gone, but the street was deserted.

"Guess your witness split," Karl said.

"You're going downtown after all." Hector's smile lit up his swarthy face.

"You want to set up someplace else while Karl runs him in?" Juliana asked. She didn't want to go to the station with Charlie.

"Sure. Let's go over to Second Avenue and see what we can catch."

"See you around, Juliana," Charlie called as Karl led him away. His eyes still sparkled.

Not if I see you first. She climbed into the van with Hector, wishing, for once, that Charlie hadn't been acting and had told the truth.

•••

"Ziffkin." Hernandez, the portly Latino booking clerk at the police station, stared at Charlie's paperwork. "Any relation to Rick Ziffkin?"

Charlie tried not to react. "Brother." How'd this cop know Rick? Last he'd heard, Rick was a police detective in Fort Lauderdale.

"Then you should know better than to solicit a prostitute."

"I wasn't."

Hernandez held up a meaty hand. "I heard the story. You're still going to cool your heels in here until we check it out."

Charlie sighed. He hadn't foreseen this delay. But then he hadn't expected to meet Juliana Sanchez in hooker clothes. After Hernandez locked him in a cell, he sat down to wait.

Juliana Sanchez. Her name melted like chocolate mint ice cream in his mouth—delectable with impact. A face of sculpted bones and those dark Sophia Loren eyes beckoned men to sin. *Mama mia*! His body still hummed with excitement, and he was still partially aroused. Wavy, dark brown hair fell to her breasts . . . and what breasts they were. Mounds to dive into and make love to for hours. They were more mouthwatering now than when she'd been sixteen and offered him his heart's desire. His palms itched to touch them. He'd had his hands on her breasts back then, but he'd swear she had more now. Maybe she had implants. No, breasts like hers were real.

Legs a man wanted wrapped around him in the throes of passion. Full pouty lips a man wanted to kiss for hours and then watch surround his cock. God, he ached for her.

She was lovelier and sexier now than she'd been when she'd captured his teenage heart. He'd thought he'd die every time he saw her. One day she was the girl next door, his best friend, the person he told all his dreams to, and the next she was . . . well, more.

Watching her walk home from the bus stop in her Catholic school uniform had given him a daily hard-on. He'd wanted to lift that plaid skirt and plunge his dick into her.

And then one day out of the blue she'd offered herself to him. He couldn't get her on her back fast enough. He'd gotten his hands inside her blouse, her panties off and his fly open before her father found them.

Charlie was lucky Sergeant Sanchez hadn't shot him. But the Sergeant had told his father, who'd given him a whipping and a lecture about good girls like Juliana. And her father had sent her away. Charlie hadn't seen her since.

Right now he felt just like he'd felt back then—aching with unfulfilled lust and regret.

"Look what the cat dragged in." His brother Rick's voice broke through his reverie.

Charlie jerked in surprise. He rose and approached the bars, his heart pounding hard in his chest. It took all his acting ability to play it cool. He'd dreaded this meeting for two years. Did his brother think the wrong brother had died? "I didn't know you were home."

"I didn't know you were either." Rick had the same dark brown hair as him, but cropped close to his head, and their father's brown eyes. He was thirty-four, four years older than Charlie, and built like a football player, like their dad.

"I flew in last night." Charlie kept his tone light. "How'd you know I was here?"

"The desk sergeant called me. What the hell were you thinking? Solicitation?" Rick spat the last word.

"I'm on a case. I was trying to get information."

"You're an actor, Charlie."

Charlie shook his head. He blamed himself for their two-year estrangement. "I gave it up."

Rick snorted. "When? You wanted to be an actor your whole life."

"I wasn't very good at it. I got tired of bit parts, four am wake-up calls, and working three jobs to pay the rent. Now people pay me to find things for them."

Rick glared at him. "C'mon, pull the other one. You'd sooner quit breathing than give up acting."

Charlie shrugged. That had been true once. Before Billy died. "Fine. Don't believe me."

"Have you seen Mom and Dad?"

Charlie looked away. "No. I told you I'm on a case. I didn't know I was going to be in town."

"Are you going to see them?"

Charlie smiled and tapped the bars. "I'm locked up at the moment."

"Still a funny man. Listen, you should see Mom and Dad while you're here. I'll call them and—"

"No!" Charlie tried to control his breathing. He couldn't face his parents yet, especially not while he was in jail. He was still building his business, and he wanted them to see him successful.

Rick used his cop stare on him, but Charlie had grown up with it, had watched it perfected. It had no effect.

"Are you avoiding something, bro?" Rick demanded.

A lot of things. "I can't waste my client's time for personal matters, Rick. He needs his property back. And sitting around in this cell isn't getting me any closer to retrieving it."

"You haven't been home in two years. It's hard to believe you couldn't spare a few days in all that time."

"New business owners have to work sixty hours a week or more. We don't get time off. And right now it's only me, so even when I'm not on a case, there's paperwork, billing, paying bills, soliciting work. And then there's the mundane personal stuff like laundry and groceries."

"I get it," Rick growled. "It doesn't have anything to do with avoiding Billy's grave."

Charlie was proud of how he controlled his flinch. Billy's death was a wound that wouldn't heal. But Charlie hadn't been an actor all those years without learning something about his craft. "I dealt with his death two years ago." When he'd changed his life. "I swear on his grave I'm on a case."

Rick sighed. "I don't understand it, but I believe you."

"How long have you been back, Rick?"

"Four months."

"And how long 'til you get antsy and leave again?"

Rick's lips quirked into a funny, silly smile. It unnerved Charlie. "I turned down a chance last week. My *wife* didn't want to move."

Charlie's world rocked on its ear. "Wife? When did you get married?"

Rick looked smug. "Two months ago." Then he sobered. "I called to invite you but you didn't answer. I left you a message."

Charlie would have remembered a call like that, but he hadn't been checking his home answering machine much. "Sorry. I told you I'm building my business." Rick looked ready to argue, so he said, "Tell me about the woman who nailed your feet to Miami."

He listened in amazement to the brother who'd pursued evidence and facts his whole life describe his wife, Analise, who allegedly saw and spoke to ghosts. And Charlie had thought there were strange people in California.

"She made me take dance lessons." Rick grimaced. "So we can dance with two of the ghosts during the full moon. It's hard not to run into the girls, since I can't see them. I try to read their location from where Analise is, but I'm wrong a lot. I hate how it feels when they float through me." He shuddered and gripped his stomach. "Analise says it's because I'm very sensitive to spiritual energy."

Charlie gaped. He could not believe the words coming out of Rick's mouth.

"But I love Analise. That's our deal—if I accept the ghosts, she'll live with me. I can't wait for you to meet her. You're going to love her. You'll love our dog, Fitz, too."

Rick had settled down with a wife and a dog. He didn't seem troubled by Billy's death or unsolved murder. Maybe when Charlie's business was a success, Billy's death would stop haunting him.

In the mood for more Crimson Romance?
Check out *Always and Forever Love* by Lynn Crandall at
CrimsonRomance.com.